THE PENGUIN BOOK OF CANADIAN FOLK SONGS

SELECTED AND EDITED BY
EDITH FOWKE

THE PENGUIN BOOK OF

Canadian Folk Songs

SELECTED AND EDITED BY

Edith Fowke

MUSIC CONSULTANT

Keith MacMillan

PENGUIN BOOKS

Penguin Books Ltd, Harmondsworth, Middlesex, England
Penguin Books Inc., 7110 Ambassador Road, Baltimore, Maryland 21207, U.S.A.
Penguin Books Australia Ltd, Ringwood, Victoria, Australia

—

First published 1973

—

Copyright © Edith Fowke, 1973

—

Printed in Great Britain by
Lowe & Brydone (Printers) Ltd, Thetford, Norfolk
Set in Monotype Times Roman
Music set by Halstan & Co. Ltd
Amersham, Bucks

CONTENTS

ACKNOWLEDGEMENTS

The Old 'Polina', The Ryans and the Pittmans, The Petty Harbour Bait Skiff, The Star of Logy Bay, An Anti-Confederation Song and *The Kelligrews Soiree* by permission of Mrs Gerald S. Doyle, St John's, Nfld.

Chanson de Louis Riel by permission of Barbara Cass-Beggs, Winnipeg, Man.

L'Habitant d'Saint-Barbe by permission of Alan Mills, Montreal, Que.

Farewell to Nova Scotia: Copyright by Gordon V. Thompson Limited, Toronto, Ont., used by permission.

The English words for *Un Canadien errant, Dans les chantiers, Ah! Si mon moine voulait danser!, En roulant ma boule, D'où viens-tu, bergère?, Vive la Canadienne!* and *C'est l'aviron* by permission of the Waterloo Music Company, Waterloo, Ontario.

Bold Wolfe by permission of Mrs Elisabeth B. Greenleaf, Westerley, R.I.

Peter Emberley, Duffy's Hotel and *The Jones Boys* by permission of Brunswick Press, Fredericton, N.B.

Harbour Le Cou, The Ferryland Sealer, Bachelor's Hall, Feller from Fortune, The Star of Belle Isle, and *She's like the Swallow:* National Museum of Man, National Museums of Canada, Bulletin 197, *Songs of the Newfoundland Outports* by K. Peacock. Reproduced by permission of Information Canada.

Mary Ann and *The False Young Man:* National Museum of Man, National Museums of Canada, Bulletin 107, *Come A-Singing!* by Marius Barbeau. Reproduced by permission of Information Canada.

INTRODUCTION

CANADIAN folk songs are not as well known as those of Britain or the United States, but they are just as numerous and singable. As I wrote in *Folk Songs of Canada*,*

'Canadian songs spring from varied and colourful sources: from the French-Canadian *habitants* who sang as they cleared their farms along the St Lawrence, and from the *coureurs-de-bois* who sang as they paddled across Canada's many waterways; from the pioneer settlers who brought to the new world the traditional ballads of England, Scotland and Ireland; from the sailors and fishermen of our maritime provinces who sang as they ran up the sails or pulled in the nets; from the prospectors of the far north, the sod-busters of the prairies, and the roving lumberjacks who sang around the shanty stoves when their day's work was done.'

The vast majority of folk songs sung in Canada were inherited from the two mother countries of France and Britain. Marius Barbeau estimated that nineteen out of twenty of all French-Canadian songs are ancient, and although there are somewhat more native English-Canadian songs, about four out of five of them also have their roots in the old land. If this book were to preserve these proportions, it would be largely a European rather than a Canadian collection; I have therefore chosen to emphasize the songs composed in Canada rather than those imported. The words of nearly all the songs in the first six sections were composed on this continent, although the tunes are largely from the British Isles or France.

Similarly, if the selection were to reflect the total number of songs collected in Canada, nearly half should be in French, but as this book is intended for an English-speaking audience, I have given only a sampling of the best known French-Canadian songs. The songs brought to this country by immigrants from other parts of the world have also enriched our national heritage, but again, as English-speaking people are not likely to sing in Ukrainian, German or Italian, the songs have been confined to the languages of our two founding races.

Some national collections group the songs by regions, but this is not practical in Canada. Most of our songs come from the eastern part of our country: Newfoundland, the Maritime provinces, Quebec and Ontario. The four western provinces were settled more recently and fewer folk songs have taken root there. Hence the west is represented only by a few

* See the Bibliography, p. 220.

samples: *Moody to the Rescue, Chanson de Louis Riel, The Red River Valley* and *The Alberta Homesteader*. The two provinces most heavily represented are Newfoundland and Ontario: Newfoundland because the isolated life of the fishermen in its tiny outports produced the greatest number of local ditties and songs of the sea, and Ontario because the lumber camps here produced the greatest number of shantyboy songs and preserved a great many fine old British ballads.

Some of our earliest native songs were inspired by events in our history, and the first section gives some samples of these. The next two sections represent the two largest groups of native Canadian songs – those composed by men who worked on the sea or in the woods. A somewhat smaller number come from those who worked on the land.

Besides those that grew out of our history and primary occupations, we have quite a few lively dance songs and amusing ditties which are grouped under the heading of 'Social Life'. The theme of love in Canada, as elsewhere, has inspired some of our most beautiful songs: it has been extended to two sections on 'True Lovers' and 'The Trials of Love'.

The last two sections give a small selection from the great wealth of British ballads that have survived in this country. Here you will find versions of some of the stories that have been most popular with Canadian folk: *The Farmer and the Devil, Jenny Go Gentle, The House Carpenter, The 'Green Willow Tree'*, and *The Sailor's Return*, along with some well known in Britain that are rare in North America: *The Dewy Dells of Yarrow, The Bonny Bunch of Rushes Green* and *Jamie Foyer*, and a few that are rare or unusual, such as *Willie Drowned in Ero, The Footboy* and *The Green Brier Shore*.

Some folklorists may question the inclusion of certain songs that have known authors, such as *The Petty Harbour Bait Skiff* or *The Kelligrews Soiree*. In England folk songs are judged by more rigid criteria than in North America. Here the tendency is to accept any song which has been taken up by the folk and sung traditionally over a considerable period of time. Nearly all the songs in this collection date back a century or more, and they have all had currency in the mouths of the folk. A number that are being printed here for the first time came direct from the singers whose names are given in the notes. Those who would like to know more about Canadian traditional singers will find brief biographies of a number of those represented (O. J. Abbott, C. H. J. Snider, Emerson Woodcock, Tom Brandon, LaRena Clark, Mrs Fraser, Albert Simms and Stanley James) in my *Traditional Singers and Songs from Ontario*.

The compiler of a popular song book is always faced with a dilemma: whether to satisfy the academic folklorists by printing songs exactly as they were collected, or to satisfy singers by modifying the words to make them more singable. I have tried to meet both demands by selecting songs that can be readily sung in their original form. Despite the strong temptation to correct obvious slips (as in verse 6 of *The House Carpenter* where the rhyme scheme shows that the first two lines have been interchanged) I have given the songs as closely as possible to the way they were sung by the traditional singers or printed by the original collectors. In one or two songs defective verses have been omitted and in a few others missing lines have been added in brackets. For the most part those who wish to sing the songs should have little trouble making their own adaptations if they find the words as printed are awkward.

The tunes also are reproduced as faithfully as possible, allowing for the fact that traditional singers rarely sing two verses exactly alike and often do not conform to the rigid metrical pattern represented by printed music. Any single representation of the tune sung by a traditional singer is almost inevitably a compromise, and no two musicians will transcribe it in exactly the same way. For those who want to know how the traditional singers did sing them, the notes indicate records that give a number of the songs as they were collected. Many Canadian singers speak the last word or phrase of a song, and these are indicated in the texts by italics.

In Canada, as in Britain, the traditional singers sang unaccompanied, and many of their songs should not have accompaniments. The old modal tunes are hard to harmonize, and often the verses are sung in a very free style which does not fit into strict rhythmical patterns, as for example, *Down by Sally's Garden*, *The Bonny Bunch of Rushes Green*, or *The Ship's Carpenter*. Keith MacMillan has given guitar chords for those which he feels would not be harmed by accompaniments. He has also transcribed a number of songs from tapes, checked all the music, and transposed some into keys more suitable for singing. I am most grateful for his careful and skilful music editing. Thanks are also due to Peggy Seeger and Vera Johnson, who transcribed some of the songs, and to Leslie Shepard, P. J. Thomas, and C. R. Vincent, who provided useful information.

I. ECHOES OF HISTORY

1. A FENIAN SONG

1. The Queen's Own Regiment was their name:
   From fair Toronto town they came
   To put the Irish all to shame –
   The Queen's and Colonel Boker!

2. What fury fills each loyal mind!
   No volunteer would stay behind.
   They flung their red rag to the wind –
   'Hurrah, my boys!' said Boker.

3. Now helter skelter Ohio,
   See how they play that 'heel and toe'!
   See how they run from their Irish foe –
   The Queen's and Colonel Boker!

2. BOLD WOLFE

1. Come all ye young men all,
   Let this delight you;
   Cheer up, you young men all,
   Let nothing fright you.
   Never let your courage fail
   When you're brought to trial,
   Nor let your fancy move
   At the first denial.

2. I went to see my love
   Thinking to woo her;
   I sat down by her side,
   Not to undo her,
   But whenever I speaks one word
   My tongue do quiver;
   I durst not speak my mind
   While I am with her.

3. 'Madame, here's a diamond ring
    If you'll accept it;
  Madame, here's a chain of gold:
    Long time I kept it,
  But when you're in repose
    Think on the giver;
  Madame, remember me,
    Undone forever.'

4. Bold Wolfe he took his leave
    From his dear jewel;
  Sorely she did lament,
    'Love, don't prove cruel.'
  He says, ' 'Tis for a space
    That I must leave you,
  But love, wher'er I go,
    I won't forget you.'

5. That brave and gallant youth
    Have crossed the ocean,
  To free America
    Of her division;
  Where he landed at Quebec
    With all his party,
  A city to attack
    Both brave and haughty.

6. Bold Wolfe drew up his men
    In a line so pretty
  On the Plains of Abraham
    Before the city:
  On the plains before the town
    Where the French did meet him;
  Where a double number round
    Is all to beat him;

7. When drawn in a line
    For death preparing
  And in each other's face
    Those two armies staring,
  Where the cannons on both sides
    Did roar like thunder,
  And youth in all their pride
    Was torn asunder;

8. Where the drums did loudly beat
    The colours a-flying,
  And the purple gore does stream
    And men lie dying . . .
  When a-shot from off his horse
    Fell that brave hero.
  May we lament his loss
    That day in sorrow.

9. (The French are seen to break,
    Their ranks are flying;)
  Bold Wolfe he seemed to wake
    As he lay dying,
  But in lifting up his head
    Where guns do rattle,
  Unto his army said,
    'How goes the battle?'

10. His aide-de-camp replied
    That 'tis in our favour,
  Quebec in all her pride
    There is none can save her.
  For 'tis falling in our hands
    With all her treasure.
  'Oh, then,' replies Bold Wolfe,
    'I will die in pleasure.'

3. THE BATTLE OF THE WINDMILL

1. On Tuesday morning we marched out
   In command of Colonel Fraser,
   With swords and bay'nets of polished steel
   As keen as any razor.
   Unto the Windmill plains we went,
   We gave them three loud cheers
   To let them know that day below
   We're the Prescott Volunteers.

2. Oh, we're the boys that feared no noise
   When the cannons loud did roar;
   We cut the rebels left and right
   When they landed on our shore.
   Brave Macdonall nobly led
   His men into the field;
   They did not flinch, no, not an inch,
   Till the rebels had to yield.

3. He swung his sword right round his head
   Saying, 'Glengarrys, follow me,
   We'll gain the day without delay,
   And that you'll plainly see!'
   The rebels now remain at home,
   We wish that they would come,
   We'd cut them up both day and night
   By command of Colonel Young.

4. If e'er they dare return again
   They'll see what we can do;
   We'll show them British play, my boys,
   As we did at Waterloo.
   Under Captain Jessup we will fight,
   Let him go where he will;
   With powder and ball they'll surely fall
   As they did at the Windmill.

5. If I were like great Virgil bright,
   I would employ my quill:
   I would write both day and night
   Concerning the Windmill.
   Lest to intrude I will conclude
   And finish off my song:
   We'll pay a visit to Ogdensburg,
   And that before it's long.

4. UN CANADIEN ERRANT

English words by Edith Fowke

Un ca - na - dien er - rant, Ban - ni de ses fo - yers, Un ca - na - dien er - rant, Ban - ni de ses fo - yers, Par - cou - rait en pleu - rant Des pa - ys é - tran - gers, Par - cou - rait en pleu - rant Des pa - ys é - tran - gers.

1. Un canadien errant
   Banni de ses foyers,
   Un canadien errant
   Banni de ses foyers,
   Parcourait en pleurant
   Des pays étrangers,
   Parcourait en pleurant
   Des pays étrangers.

2. Un jour, triste et pensif, ⎱ 2
   Assis au bord des flots, ⎰
   Au courant fugitif ⎱ 2
   Il adressa ces mots: ⎰

3. Si tu vois mon pays, ⎱ 2
   Mon pays malheureux, ⎰
   Va, dis à mes amis ⎱
   Que je me souviens d'eux. ⎰ 2

1. Once a Canadian lad,
   Exiled from hearth and home,
   Wandered, alone and sad,
   Through alien lands unknown.
   Down by a rushing stream,
   Thoughtful and sad one day,
   He watched the water pass
   And to it he did say:

2. 'If you should reach my land,
   My most unhappy land,
   Please speak to all my friends
   So they will understand.
   Tell them how much I wish
   That I could be once more
   In my beloved land
   That I will see no more.

4. Ô jours si pleins d'appas } 2
    Vous êtes disparus . . .
    Et ma patrie, hélas! } 2
    Je ne la verrai plus!

5. Non, mais en expirant, } 2
    Ô mon cher Canada!
    Mon regard languissant } 2
    Vers toi se portera.

3. 'My own beloved land
   I'll not forget till death,
   And I will speak of her
   With my last dying breath.
   My own beloved land
   I'll not forget till death,
   And I will speak of her
   With my last dying breath.'

5. MOODY TO THE RESCUE

Word came down to Der - by town In the
spring of 'fif - ty - nine : Mc - Go - wan's men had
smashed the pen And left for the Hill's Bar
Mine. *Ri - cky doo dum day, doo dum day,*
Ri - cky di - cky doo dum day.

1. Word came down to Derby town
   In the spring of 'fifty-nine:
   McGowan's men had smashed the
      pen
   And left for the Hill's Bar Mine.

   CHORUS:
   Ricky doo dum day, doo dum day,
   Ricky dicky doo dum day.

2. 'I say by gad, now things look bad!
   I'll tell you what we'll do.
   Captain Grant take twenty-five men
   And I'll come along with you.'

3. Through all that night bold Captain
      Wright
   Took Moody and his men
   On the *Enterprise* 'neath frosty skies
   To Hope and came back again.

24

4. To the warlike scene came a hundred
     marines
   With boys of jackets blue
   From the *Satellite* prepared to fight
   Or see what they could do.

5. They did not fail: they came to Yale
   But things were nice and quiet.
   On the Sabbath day the miners pray
   And didn't wish to fight.

6. 'Things look all right so where's the
     fight?'
   Said Moody to his men.
   'We'll cut it short and make the
     report
   And then get back again.'

7. Let's drink a health to the miners
     bold,
   To Moody and his men.
   If McGowan ever steps out of line
   We'll call them back again.

6. BY THE HUSH, ME BOYS

Oh, it's by the hush, me boys, I'm sure that's to hold your noise, And lis - ten to poor Pad - dy's nar - ra - tion. I___ was by hun - ger pressed and in po - ver - ty dis - tressed, So I took a thought I'd leave the I - rish na - tion. *Here's you, boys, do take my ad - vice, To A - me - ri - cay I'd have yous not be com - ing. There is no-thing here but war where the mur-der-ing can-nons roar, And I wish I was at home in dear old Er - eein.*

1. Oh, it's by the hush, me boys, I'm sure that's to hold your noise,
   And listen to poor Paddy's narration.
   I was by hunger pressed and in poverty distressed,
   So I took a thought I'd leave the Irish nation.

CHORUS:

> *Here's you, boys, do take my advice,*
> *To Americay I'd have yous not be coming.*
> *There is nothing here but war where the murdering cannons roar,*
> *And I wish I was at home in dear old Ereein.*

2. Then I sold my horse and plough, me little pigs and cow,
   And me little farm of land and I parted,
   And me sweetheart Biddy Magee I'm afeared I'll never see,
   For I left her that morning broken-hearted.

3. Then meself and a hundred more to Americay sailed o'er,
   Our fortune to be making we were thinking.
   When we landed in Yankee land, shoved a gun into our hand,
   Saying, 'Paddy, you must go and fight for Lincoln.'

4. General Mahar to us said, 'If you get shot or lose your head,
   Every murdered soul of you will get a pension.'
   In the war I lost me leg; all I've now is a wooden peg;
   By me soul it is the truth to you I mention.

5. Now I think meself in luck to be fed upon Indian buck
   In old Ireland, the country I delight in,
   And with the devil I do say, 'Curse Americay,'
   For I'm sure I've got enough of their hard fighting.

7. AN ANTI-CONFEDERATION SONG

Hur – rah for our own na - tive isle, New-found - land!___
___ Not a stran-ger shall hold___ one inch of its
strand!_____ Her face turns to Bri - tain, her
back to the Gulf. _____ Come near at your
pe - ril, Ca - na - di - an Wolf!_____

(Note: The tune would be improved by eliminating the sharps.)

1. Hurrah for our own native isle, Newfoundland!
   Not a stranger shall hold one inch of its strand!
   Her face turns to Britain, her back to the Gulf.
   Come near at your peril, Canadian Wolf!

2. Ye brave Newfoundlanders who plough the salt sea
   With hearts like the eagle so bold and so free,
   The time is at hand when you'll all have to say
   If Confederation will carry the day.

3. Cheap tea and molasses they say they will give,
   All taxes take off that the poor man may live:
   Cheap nails and cheap lumber our coffins to make,
   And homespun to mend our old clothes when they break.

4. If they take off the taxes how then will they meet
   The heavy expense of the country's up-keep?
   Just give them the chance to get us in the scrape
   And they'll chain you as slaves with pen, ink and red tape.

5. Would you barter the right that your fathers have won,
   Your freedom transmitted from father to son?
   For a few thousand dollars of Canadian gold
   Don't let it be said that your birthright was sold!

8. CHANSON DE LOUIS RIEL

English words by Barbara Cass-Beggs

C'est au champ de ba-tai - lle J'ai fait é-crir' dou-leurs. On cou-che sur la pai - lle, Ça fait fré-mir les coeurs. Or je r' - çois t'une let - tre De ma chè-re ma - man. J'a-vais ni plum' ni en - cre Pour pou-voir lui z'é-crire. Or je pris mon ca - nif, Je le trem - pis dans mon sang, Pour é-crir' t'un vieu' let - tre À ma chè-re ma - man.

1. C'est au champ de bataille
   J'ai fait écrir' douleurs.
   On couche sur la paille,
   Ça fait frémir les cœurs.

2. Or je r'çois t'une lettre
   De ma chère maman.
   J'avais ni plum' ni encre
   Pour pouvoir lui z'écrire.

3. Or je pris mon canif,
   Je le trempis dans mon sang,
   Pour écrir' t'un vieu' lettre
   À ma chère maman.

4. Quand ell' r'cevra cett' lettre
   Toute écrit' de sang,
   Ses yeux baignant de larmes,
   Son cœur sera mourant.

5. S'y jett' à genoux par terre
   En appelant ses enfants:
   Priez pour votre frère
   Qui est au régiment.

6. Mourir, s'il faut mourir,
   Chacun meurt à son tour;
   J'aim' mieux mourir en brave,
   Faut tous mourir un jour.

1. I send this letter to you
   To tell my grief and pain,
   And as I lie imprisoned
   I long to see again

2. You, my beloved mother,
   And all my comrades dear.
   I write these words in my heart's
      blood:
   No ink or pen is here.

3. My friends in arms and children,
   Please weep and pray for me.
   I fought to keep our country
   So that we might be free.

4. When you receive this letter
   Please weep for me and pray
   That I may die with bravery
   Upon that fearful day.

II. THE SEA

9. THE 'FLYING CLOUD'

My name is Ed-ward _ Hol-land as _ you might un-der-stand. I was born, brought up in Wa-ter-ford's town in _ E-rin's hap-py land. When I was young and in my prime, kind _ for-tune on me smiled; My pa-rents do-ted on _ me, I _ being their _ on-ly child.

1. My name is Edward Holland as you might understand.
   I was born, brought up in Waterford's town in Erin's happy land.
   When I was young and in my prime, kind fortune on me smiled;
   My parents doted on me, I being their only child.

2. My father bound me to a trade in Waterford's fair town.
   He bound me to a cooper there by the name of William Brown.
   I served my master faithfully for eighteen months or more,
   Till I shipped on board of the *Ocean Queen* sailing for Belfraser's shore.

3. Now when we reached Belfraser's shore I met with Captain Moore,
   The commander of the *Flying Cloud* sailing out from Baltimore.
   He wanted me to come with him, on a slaving voyage to go
   To the burning plains of Africa where the sugar-cane does grow.

4. The *Flying Cloud* was a clipper barge carrying eighty tons or more;
   She could easily sail round anything coming out from Baltimore.
   Her sails were as white as the driven snow and on them was no stain,
   And eighteen mounted polished guns she carried a b aft her main.

34

5. So we sailed away o'er the raging main till we came to the African shores.
   Five hundred of those poor black souls from their native homes we tore;
   We dragged them all across our decks and stowed them down below,
   And eighteen inches to a man was all that we could allow.

6. We sailed away o'er the raging main with a full cargo of slaves.
   It would have been better for those poor souls had they been in their graves,
   For the plague and fever came on board, swept half of them away;
   We dragged their bodies across our decks and hove them in the sea.

7. So we sailed away all gallant gay till we came to the Cuban shores
   And sold them to the planters there to be slaves forever more,
   To work all day in the cotton fields beneath the blazing sun,
   To while away their few short hours till their life's race was run.

8. [But soon our money it was all spent, we put to sea again;]
   Then Captain Moore he came on deck and said to us, his men:
   'There is gold and silver to be had if with me you'll remain.
   We'll hoist aloft the pirate flag and scour the Spanish Main.'

9. We all agreed but five of us who asked to be put on land;
   Two of them were Boston boys and two from Newfoundland,
   The other was an Irish youth who had sailed out from Tramore.
   How I wished to God I had joined those boys and returned with them to shore!

10. Now the *Flying Cloud* was as clever a ship as ever swam the seas,
    Or ever hoisted a main topsail before a lively breeze.
    I have often seen that gallant ship as the wind lay abaft her wheel,
    With her royal and sky sails set aloft, taking nineteen from her keel.

11. We robbed and plundered many a ship down on the Spanish Main,
    Caused many the poor widow and orphan child in sorrow to remain.
    We made their crews to walk our planks and they hung from out our sails,
    For the saying of our skipper was that a dead man tells no tales.

12. We were pursued by frigates fast and ships of the Lion, too.
    It was always far astern of us their bursting shells they threw.
    It was always far astern of us their cannon boomed aloud;
    There was many tried, but all in vain, to catch the *Flying Cloud*.

13. Till at last the Spanish man-of-war, the *Dungeon*, hove in view;
    She fired a shot across our bow as a signal to heave to.
    We paid to her but little heed and ran before the wind,
    When a chain-shot cut our main-mast down and then we fell behind.

14. We cleared our decks for action as they hauled up 'longside,
    And right across our quarterdeck they poured a leaden tide.
    We fought till Captain Moore was shot and eighty of his men;
    When a chain-shot set our ship on fire, we were forced to surrender then.

15. We were taken prisoners, into a prison cast,
    To be tried and found guilty and to be hung at last.
    It was drinking and bad company that made this wreck of me;
    Have pity on my fate, my boys, and curse this piracy.

16. Here's adieu unto that colleen fair, the girl I left behind;
    Her heart would break if she knew I have come to this sad end.
    No more will I kiss her ruby lips or hold her lily-white hand;
    On the gallows high now I must die by the laws of the Spanish land.

10. THE LOSS OF THE 'ELLEN MUNN'

Oh, it hap-pened to be on Christ-mas day, 'Twas from King's Cove — we sailed a-way, As we were bound up to Goose Bay — The *El-len* to re-pair.— When we left the wind was down, We head-ed her up for New-man's Sound, The *El-len*, my boys, she did lose ground, Fell off for Lit-tle De-nier.

1. Oh, it happened to be on Christmas day,
   'Twas from King's Cove we sailed away,
   As we were bound up to Goose Bay
     The *Ellen* to repair.
   When we left the wind was down,
   We headed her up for Newman's Sound,
   The *Ellen*, my boys, she did lose ground,
     Fell off for Little Denier.

2. The wind veered to the west-sou'west
   And Barrow Harbour we could not fetch.
   The gale grew blustering down the retch –
       'Twas near the close of day.
   So to Dark Hole we ran her in,
   And waited there for a half-free wind,
   The twenty-seventh to begin
       Our anchors for to weigh.

3. Next morning then our hearts were light,
   We ran her up for the standing ice
   Thinking that all things were right
       As you may understand.
   Till from below there came a roar:
   'There's water up to the cabin floor.'
   The signals of distress did soar
       For help from off the land.

4. The men into the hold did make,
   The women to the pumps did take
   In hopes that they might stop the leak
       And beach her in a trice.
   But water still came tumbling in –
   Against the flow we could not win.
   The Skipper's voice rose o'er the din:
       'All hands get on the ice.'

5. Now to our very sad mistake
   We found the ice was very weak.
   We had to carry and to take
       The children to dry ground.
   Poor Tommy Rolland scratched his head:
   'For God's sake, Skipper, save me bed!'
   Immediately the words were said
       The *Ellen* she went down.

6. Early next morning we bid adieu
   To bring down Tommy Rolland's crew.
   We landed them in Plate Cove too
       For to walk down the shore.
   Repeating often he did say:
   'I'll never be caught up in Goose Bay.
   If I get out of it today
       I'll trouble it no more.'

7. Tom Holloway lives on Goose Bay shore,
His father and two brothers more –
All hardy men to ply an oar –
   Westward that day did wend.
A pair of boots, a barrel of flour
They salvaged working half an hour,
And leather for Joe Horney for
   Susannah's boots to mend.

8. And now to close take this advice:
Don't ever trust the new-made ice.
'Twill hold and squeeze you like a vice,
   'Twill shave your planks away,
Till finally they're cut so thin
Through your seam the seas come in,
And when a sea voyage you begin,
   Don't sail on Christmas day.

11. THE BANKS OF NEWFOUNDLAND

Oh, — ye may— bless your hap-py lots, all— ye who dwell on shore, For it's lit-tle ye know of— the hard-ships that we poor sea-men [b]ore. It's— lit-tle ye know of— the hard-ships that we were forced to stand For— four-teen days and— fif-teen nights on the banks of New-found-land.

1. Oh, ye may bless your happy lots, all ye who dwell on shore,
   For it's little ye know of the hardships that we poor seamen [b]ore.
   It's little ye know of the hardships that we were forced to stand
   For fourteen days and fifteen nights on the banks of Newfoundland.

2. Our ship she sailed through frost and snow from the day we left Quebec,
   And if we had not walked about we'd have frozen to the deck,
   But we being true-born sailormen as ever a ship had manned,
   Our captain doubled our grog each day on the banks of Newfoundland.

3. There never was a ship, my boys, that sailed the western sea
   But the billowy waves came rolling in and bent them into staves.
   Our ship being built of unseasoned wood and could but little stand,
   The hurricane it met us there on the banks of Newfoundland.

4. We fasted for three days and nights, our provisions giving out.
   On the morning of the fourth day, we cast our lots about.
   The lot it fell on the captain's son; thinking relief at hand,
   We spared him for another night on the banks of Newfoundland.

5. On the morning of the fifth day no vessel did appear.
   We gave to him another hour to offer up a prayer,
   But Providence to us proved kind, kept blood from every hand,
   For an English vessel hove in sight on the banks of Newfoundland.

6. We hoisted aloft our signal; they bore down on us straightway.
   When they saw our pitiful condition, they began to weep and pray.
   Five hundred souls we had on board the day we left the land:
   There's now alive but seventy-five on the banks of Newfoundland.

7. They took us off of the wreck, my boys; we were more like ghosts than men.
   They fed us and they clothed us and brought us back again.
   They fed us and they clothed us and brought us safe to land,
   While the billowy waves roll o'er their graves on the banks of Newfound*land*.

12. THE RYANS AND THE PITTMANS

We'll rant and we'll roar __ like true New-found-lan-ders, We'll rant and we'll roar on deck and be-low Un-til we see bot-tom in-side the two sunk-ers, When straight through the Chan-nel to Tos-low we'll go.

1. My name it is Robert, they call me Bob Pittman;
   I sail in the *Ino* with Skipper Tim Brown.
   I'm bound to have Dolly or Biddy or Molly
   As soon as I'm able to plank the cash down.

CHORUS:
   We'll rant and we'll roar like true Newfoundlanders,
   We'll rant and we'll roar on deck and below
   Until we see bottom inside the two sunkers,
   When straight through the Channel to Toslow we'll go.

2. I'm a son of a sea-cook, and a cook in a trader;
   I can dance, I can sing, I can reef the main-boom;
   I can handle a jigger, and cuts a big figure
   Whenever I gets in a boat's standing room.

3. If the voyage is good, then this fall I will do it;
   I wants two pound ten for a ring and the priest,
   A couple o' dollars for clean shirt and collars,
   And a handful o' coppers to make up a feast.

4. There's plump little Polly, her name is Goldsworthy;
   There's John Coady's Kitty, and Mary Tibbo;
   There's Clara from Bruley, and young Martha Foley,
   But the nicest of all is my girl in Toslow.

5. Farewell and adieu to ye fair ones of Valen,
   Farewell and adieu to ye girls in the Cove;
   I'm bound to the westward, to the wall with the hole in,
   I'll take her from Toslow the wild world to rove.

6. Farewell and adieu to ye girls of St Kyran's,
   Of Paradise and Presque, Big and Little Bona,
   I'm bound unto Toslow to marry sweet Biddy,
   And if I don't do so, I'm afraid of her da.

7. I've bought me a house from Katherine Davis,
   A twenty-pound bed from Jimmy McGrath;
   I'll get me a settle, a pot and a kettle;
   Then I'll be ready for Biddy – hurrah!

8. I bought in the *Ino* this spring from the city
   Some rings and gold brooches for the girls in the Bay;
   I bought me a case-pipe – they call it a meerschaum –
   It melted like butter upon a hot day.

9. I went to a dance one night at Fox Harbour;
   There were plenty of girls, so nice as you'd wish;
   There was one pretty maiden a-chawing of frankgum,
   Just like a young kitten a-gnawing fresh fish.

10. Then here is a health to the girls of Fox Harbour,
    Of Oderin and Presque, Crabbes Hole and Bruley.
    Now let ye be jolly, don't be melancholy;
    I can't marry all, or in chokey I'd be.

13. THE PETTY HARBOUR BAIT SKIFF

1. Good people all both great and small, I hope you will attend,
   And listen to these verses few that I have lately penned,
   And I'll relate the hardships great that fishermen must stand
   While fighting for a livelihood on the coast of Newfoundland.

2. It happened to be in the summer time in the lovely month of June,
   When fields were green, fair to be seen, and valleys were in bloom,
   When silent fountains do run clear, caressed by Heaven's rain,
   And the dewy showers that fall at night do fertilize the plain.

3. We bid adieu unto our friends and those we hold most dear,
   Being bound from Petty Harbour in the springtime of the year.
   The little birds, as we sailed on, sung o'er the hills and dales,
   While Flora from her sportive groves sent forth her pleasant gales.

4. On Saturday we sailed away, being in the evening late,
   Bound into Conception Bay all for a load of bait.
   The seagulls flying in the air and pitching on the shore,
   But little we thought 'twould be our lot to see our friends no more.

5. The weather being fine we lost no time until we were homeward bound;
   The whales were sporting in the deep and the swordfish swimming round,
   And Luna bright shone forth that night to illuminate the 'say',
   And the stars shone bright to guide us right upon our rude pathway.

6. We shook our reefs and trimmed our sails, across the bay did stand;
   The sun did rise, all circleized, like streamers o'er the land.
   The clouds lay in the atmosphere, for our destruction met,
   Boreas blew a heavy squall, our boat was overset.

7. When we came to the 'Nor'ad' head, a rainbow did appear,
   There was every indication that a storm was drawing near.
   Old Neptune riding on the ways, to windward of us lay;
   You'd think the ocean was on fire in Petty Harbour Bay.

8. John French was our commander, Mick Sullivan second hand,
   And all the rest were brave young men reared up in Newfoundland.
   Six brave youths, to tell the truth, were buried in the sea,
   But the Lord preserved young Menshon's life for to live a longer day.

9. Your heart would ache all for their sake if you were standing by,
   To see them drowning one by one, and no relief being nigh;
   Struggling with the boisterous waves all in their youth and bloom,
   But at last they sank to rise no more, all on the eighth of June.

10. Jacob Chafe, that hero brave and champion on that day,
    They boldly launched their boat with speed and quickly put to sea.
    They saved young Menshon from the wreck by their united skill;
    Their efforts would be all in vain but for kind Heaven's will.

11. Out of that fine young crew you know, there was one escaped being drowned.
    He was brought to Petty Harbour where good comforts there he found.
    He is now on shore and safe once more, with no cause to complain.
    He fought old Neptune up and down whilst on the stormy main.

12. When the sad news arrived next day in dear old St John's town,
    There was crying and lamenting on the streets both up and down.
    Their mothers were lamenting, crying for those they bore.
    On the boisterous waves they found their graves where they ne'er shall see more.

13. Now to conclude and finish these few lines I write in pain:
    Never depend out of your strength while sailing on the main,
    But put your trust in Providence, observe the Lord's command,
    And He'll guard you right, both day and night, upon the sea and land.

14. THE WRECK OF THE 'MARY SUMMERS'

Oh, the *Ma-ry Sum-mers* as you will see Load-ed in St An-drew's for the old coun-trie. She load-ed deals and__ lob-sters too, And shipped fine men for to make her crew.

1. Oh, the *Mary Summers* as you will see
   Loaded in St Andrews for the old countrie.
   She loaded deals and lobsters too,
   And shipped fine men for to make her crew.

2. Across the Banks we soon did steer
   And shipped our course for old Cape Clear.
   We worked her with the greatest ease,
   And made the run in thirty days.

3. Now we are lying in Liverpool,
   Bound back for Boston with gas coal.
   Soon out of the Channel we shall steer
   And bid adieu to old Cape Clear.

4. But the *Summers* meets with a heavy gale
   And springs a leak under close-reefed sail,
   With her bowsprit gone and her rudder too,
   And soon we'll be a used-up crew.

5. Six days we pumped her with a will,
   While thoughts of home our hearts did fill.
   On the seventh morn our pumps did sound:
   Nine feet of water in the hold was found.

6. But in the morning we can see
   The *William Bradley* upon our lee.
   We all stood by and did wear her round
   And set our colours union down.

7. And as the *Bradley* did draw near
   And close across our quarters steer,
   We hailed her as she did go past:
   Our captain said, 'We're sinking
      fast.'

8. Then our captain says to every man:
   'Swing out the boats; save all you
      can.
   Save all you can, lower the boats
      away,
   And on this wreck we'll no longer
      stay.'

9. Then into the boats we all did get,
   Not thinking of the cold or wet.
   On the *Bradley*'s deck we soon did
      stand
   To be welcomed there by every man.

10. Now the *Bradley*'s crew was eight,
      I mean
   Before our crew made up nineteen,
   And our grub being short and our
      water low,
   Into some port in Spain we'll go.

11. Now to the sorrow of our hearts
   In this port of Cadiz we must part.
   Oh, some will go and some
      remain –
   Good luck to all till we meet again!

15. THE OLD 'POLINA'

1. There's a noble fleet of whalers a-sailing from Dundee,
   Manned by British sailors to take them o'er the sea.
   On a western ocean passage we started on the trip,
   And we flew along just like a song in our gallant whaling ship.

CHORUS:
> *For the wind was on her quarter and the engines working free,*
> *There's not another whaler that sails the Arctic Sea*
> *Can beat the old 'Polina', you need not try, my sons,*
> *For we challenged all both great and small from Dundee to St John's.*

2. 'Twas the second Sunday morning just after leaving port,
   We met a heavy sou'west gale that washed away our boat,
   It washed away our quarter-deck, our stanchions just as well,
   And so we set the whole 'she-bang' a-floating in the gale.

3. Art Jackson set his canvas, Fairweather got up steam,
   And Captain Guy, the daring b'y, came plunging through the stream,
   And Mullins in the *Husky* tried to beat the blooming lot,
   But to beat the old *Polina* was something he could not.

4. There's the noble *Terra Nova*, a model without doubt,
   The *Arctic* and *Aurora* they talk so much about,
   Art Jackman's model mail-boat – the terror of the sea –
   Tried to beat the old *Polina* on a passage from Dundee.

5. And now we're back in old St John's, where rum is very cheap,
   So we'll drink a health to Captain Guy who brought us o'er the deep,
   A health to all our sweethearts and to our wives so fair;
   Not another ship could make the trip with the *Polina*, I declare.

16. THE FERRYLAND SEALER

1. Oh, our schooner and our sloop in Ferryland they do lie:
They are already riggèd to be bound for the ice.
All you lads of the Southern we will have you to beware:
She is going to the ice in the spring of the year.

CHORUS:
Laddie whack fall the laddie, laddie whack fall the day.

2. We had vittles for to last more than two months at the least,
   And plenty of good rum, boys, stowed away in our chest.
   We will give her a rally for to praise all our fancy,
   All our seals will be collected by the *William* and the *Nancy*.

3. Our course be east-north-east for two days and two nights;
   Our captain he cried out, 'Boys, look ahead for the ice!'
   And we hove her about standing in for the land,
   And 'twas in a few hours we were firm in the jam.

4. Oh, our captain he cried out, 'Come on, boys, and bear a hand!'
   Our cook he gets the breakfast and each man takes a dram.
   With their bats in their hands it was earlye to go,
   Every man showed his action 'thout the missing of a blow.

5. Some were killing, some were scalping, some were hauling on board,
   And some more they were firing and a-missing of their loads.
   In the dusk of the evening all hands in from the cold,
   And we counted nine hundred fine scalps in the hold.

6. Oh, now we are loaded and our schooner she is sound,
   And the ice it is open and to Ferryland we're bound.
   We all gave her a rally for to praise all our fancy:
   Our seals they were collected by the *William* and the *Nancy*.

7. We are now off Cape Spear and in sight of Cape Broyle:
   We will dance, sing, carouse, my boys, in just a little while.
   We will soon enjoy the charms of our sweethearts and friends,
   For it will not be long before we're down to the bend.

17. HARD, HARD TIMES

1. So now I'm intending to sing you a song
   About the poor people, how they get along.
   They start in the spring and they work till the fall,
   And when they clew up they have nothing at all,

CHORUS:
   And it's hard, hard times.

2. You start with the jigger the first in the spring,
   And across the gunnel you'll make the lines sing;
   Perhaps lose your jigger, get froze with the cold,
   Now that's the first starting of going in the hole . . .

3. It's out with the traps and the trawls too likewise,
   Perhaps get a kentle, a good sign for the voyage.
   You'll feel up in spirits and work with a will –
   Next morning adrift, you've gone in the hole still . . .

4. When so much is caught and then put out to dry
   The next is the trouble to keep off the flies.
   It's buzz all around, more trouble for you –
   Then out shines the sun and it's split right in two . . .

5. Then here comes the schooners – go get your supplies;
   A good price this summer – just make it good, b'ys.
   Seven for the large fish and five for the small,
   Pick out your West Indies and wait till the fall . . .

6. Then here comes the carpenter, he will build you a house:
   He will build it so snug that you'll scarce see a mouse.
   There'll be leaks in the roof, there'll be holes in the floor,
   The chimney will smoke, and it's open the door . . .

7. The next comes the doctor, the worst of them all,
   Saying, 'What is the matter with you all the fall?'
   He says he will cure you of all your disease –
   When he gets all your money, you can die if you please . . .

8. But never mind, friends, let us work with a will.
   When we finish down here we'll be hauled on the hill,
   And there they will lay us down deep in the cold –
   When all here is finished, you're still in the hole . . .

18. TAKING GAIR IN THE NIGHT

1. Come all you good people, come listen you might,
   It's only a ditty I'm going to write.
   It's only a ditty, I'm sure it's all right:
   It's all about taking your gair in the night.

2. John Keeping came up here to give the first call,
   And with a loud shout those words he did bawl:
   'Heave out, jolly boys! It's a beautiful night!
   All hands are bound out taking gair in the night!'

3. The first tick of engine, I think 'twas the *Slick*,
   Went pushing out through with a mightiful tick.
   With the moon up above and the stars shining bright,
   All hands are bound out taking gair in the night.

4. Sam said to Hughie, 'It's a beautiful night.'
   'Darn it,' said Hughie, 'no doubt it's all right.'
   They put on their oilskins at one in the night;
   Those boys were bound out taking gair in the night.

5. The next man to mention it was little Foss;
   He left about three o'clock to go across.
   The wind from the south-east it came on to blow,
   And back to the Island little Fossie did go.

6. You'll talk of your soldiers, the battles do fight,
   The same of your sailors who do all their might.
   I'll put it in print, you can say what you like:
   Brave-O to the man who takes gair in the night!

7. They work on the sea a living to earn,
   And not for a squall those boys will not turn.
   They'll venture their lives their families to keep,
   When stormy winds blow and the billows do leap.

8. Jerry Fudge is my name, 'twas I made the song;
   I'll sing it to you, boys, it won't take me long.
   I'll sing it to you, it's the best I can do;
   There's nobody knows what hardships I've been through.

9. I have been fishing, I know what it's like,
   But never did I take my gair in the night,
   And now I'm not fishing, I'm keeping the light.
   Cheerio to the man who takes gair in the night!

10. Come all you young ladies, I'll have you to know,
    Don't ever despise a fisherman bold,
    But huddle and cuddle, fond lovers' delight;
    They'll tell you about taking gair in the night.

11. Now to conclude and to finish my song,
    The boys from the Island they soon will be gone.
    They're going to spend Christmas with fond lovers' delight,
    And that won't be out taking gair in the night.

12. Now fishing's all over so late in the fall,
    The boys are bound homeward to drink their alc'hol,
    And as they were leaving, I heard them all say:
    'Farewell to Penguin Island while we are away.'

19. FAREWELL TO NOVA SCOTIA

The sun was set-ting___ in the___ west, The___
birds were sing-ing on ev-'ry___ tree, All___
na-ture seemed in-clined for___ rest, But___
still___ there___ was___ no___ rest for me. *Fare-*
-well to No-va Sco-tia, the sea-bound coast, Let your
moun-tains dark and drea-ry___ be, For when
I am far a-way on the bri-ny o-cean tossed, Will you
e-ver heave a sigh___ and a wish for me?

1. The sun was setting in the west,
   The birds were singing on ev'ry tree,
   All nature seemed inclined for rest,
   But still there was no rest for me.

CHORUS:

> Farewell to Nova Scotia, the sea-bound coast,
> Let your mountains dark and dreary be,
> For when I am far away on the briny ocean tossed,
> Will you ever heave a sigh and a wish for me?

2. I grieve to leave my native land,
   I grieve to leave my comrades all,
   And my agèd parents whom I always held so dear,
   And the bonny, bonny lass that I do adore.

3. The drums they do beat and the wars do alarm,
   The captain calls, we must obey,
   So farewell, farewell to Nova Scotia's charms,
   For it's early in the morning I am far, far away.

4. I have three brothers and they are at rest,
   Their arms are folded on their breast,
   But a poor simple sailor just like me
   Must be tossed and driven on the dark blue sea.

III. THE WOODS

20. HOGAN'S LAKE

1. Oh, come all you brisk young fellows that assemble here tonight,
   Assist my bold endeavours while these few lines I write.
   It's of a gang of shantyboys I mean to let you know,
   They went up for Thomas Laugheren through storm, frost and snow.

2. 'Twas up on the Black River at a place called Hogan's Lake
   Those able-bodied fellows went square timber for to make.
   The echo of their axes rung from shore to shore –
   The lofty pine they fell so fast, like cannons they did roar.

3. There were two gangs of scorers, their names I do not mind.
   They ranged the mountains o'er and o'er their winter's work to find.
   They tossed the pine both right and left, the blocks and slivers flew –
   They scared the wild moose from their yards, likewise the caribou.

4. Our hewers they were tasty and they ground their axes fair –
   They aimed their blows so neatly I am sure they'd split a hair.
   They followed up the scorers, they were not left behind –
   To do good work I really think all hands are well inclined.

5. Bill Hogan was our hewer's name, I mean to let you know –
   Full fourteen inches of the line he'd split with every blow.
   He swung his axe so freely, he done his work so clean,
   If you saw the timber hewed by him, you'd swear he used a plane.

6. Tom Hogan was our foreman's name, and very well he knew
   How to conduct his business and what shantyboys should do.
   He knew when timber was well made, when teams they had good loads,
   How to lay it up and to swamp it out, and how men should cut the roads.

7. At four o'clock in the morning the teamsters would awake.
   They'd go out and feed their horses; then their breakfasts they would take.
   'Turn out, me boys ' the foreman cries when each horse is on the road.
   'You must away before 'tis day, those teams for to unload.'

8. If you were in the shanty when they came in at night,
   To see them dance, to hear them sing, it would your heart delight.
   Some asked for patriotic songs; some for love songs did call.
   Fitzsimmons sung about the girl that wore the waterfall.

21. THE LAKE OF THE CAOGAMA

1. Oh, now we're leaving home, me boys; to Ottawa we're goin',
   Expecting to get hired, and yet we do not know.
   We met with old Tom Patterson, sayin', 'Ain't you goin' awa'?'
   'I'm goin' up the Gatineau River round the lake of the Caogama.'

2. Oh, now we're leaving Ottawa in sorrow, grief and woe;
   We're going to a place, to a place we do not know.
   We've fifty miles to travel and hard biscuits for to chaw –
   May the devil take old Patterson and the lake of the Caogama!

3. Oh, now we're in the shanty, no comfort can we find.
   We're thinking of our own dear girls, the ones we left behind,
   And dreamed at night they visit us, and their merry face we saw
   Until we woke broken-hearted round the lake of the Caogama.

4. Oh, we'll all be down in April – that's if we are alive,
   If Paddy doesn't keep us on the cursed creeks to drive.
   There's big lakes and small lakes and lakes you never saw,
   But the darnedest lake among them is the lake of the Caogama.

1. Oh, come all you boys that wish to hear
   How we got up to the woods last year.
   For Arnprior we set out
   All with John Pratt to show us the route.

   CHORUS:
   To me rant a-na, fall the doo-a-da,
   Rant and roar and drunk on the way.

2. Oh, into the buggy we jugged our boots,
   You bet our teamster fed long oats.
   As through the town we drove along,
   We all joined up in a sing-song.

3. Old Mills came out to welcome us in,
   He handed us down the wine and gin.
   The landlord's treat went merrily around
   And we drank a health to Dacre town.

4. Oh, you may depend that we felt big:
    We were in a silver-mounted rig.
    For Dacre town we hoisted our sails
    And they all thought we were the Prince of Wales.

5. Oh, supper being ready, we all took seats.
    Of course our foreman he said grace.
    Johnny Morin thought long to wait
    And Laderoute Joe shoved up his plate.

6. Oh, there was Albert Tapp and Jack McCann;
    You know he was our handy man.
    The rest of our crew you all do know:
    There was John Pratt and Laderoute Joe.

23. DANS LES CHANTIERS

English words by Edith Fowke

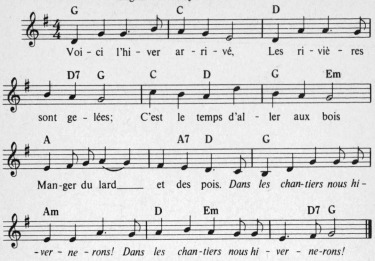

Voi - ci l'hi - ver ar - ri - vé, Les ri - viè - res sont ge - lées; C'est le temps d'al - ler aux bois Man-ger du lard___ et des pois. *Dans les chan-tiers nous hi - -ver - ne - rons! Dans les chan-tiers nous hi - ver - ne-rons!*

1. Voici l'hiver arrivé,
   Les rivières sont gelées;
   C'est le temps d'aller aux bois
   Manger du lard et des pois.

   REFRAIN:
   Dans les chantiers nous hivernerons!
   Dans les chantiers nous hivernerons!

2. Pauv' voyageur, que t'as d'la
      misère!
   Souvent tu couches par terre;
   À la pluie, au mauvais temps,
   À la rigueur de tous les temps!

3. Quand tu arriv' à Québec,
   Souvent tu fais un gros bec.
   Tu vas trouver ton bourgeois
   Qu'est là assis à son comptoi'.

4. Je voudrais être payé
   Pour le temps que j'ai donné.
   Quand l'bourgeois est en
      banq'route,
   Il te renvoi' manger des croûtes.

1. When the winter comes at last
   And the river freezes fast,
   Out into the woods we go,
   Live for months there in the snow.

   CHORUS:
   Away we go to the winter camp!
   Away we go to the winter camp!

2. Wretched man, what lies ahead?
   On the ground you'll make your bed.
   In the rain or in the snow,
   Cold hard work is all you'll know.

3. When you reach Quebec next spring
   Aching bones are all you'll bring.
   First to see the boss you head,
   Ask for cash to buy your bread.

4. When you ask him to be paid
   For the days that you have slaved,
   If he tells you he is broke,
   You won't laugh much at his joke.

5. Quand tu retourn' chez ton père,
   Aussi pour revoir ta mère,
   Le bonhomme est à la porte,
   La bonn' femme fait la gargotte.

6. Ah! bonjour donc, mon cher
      enfant!
    Nous apport'-tu bien d'l'argent?
    Que l'diable emport' les chantiers!
    Jamais d'ma vie j'y r'tournerai!

DERNIER REFRAIN:
    Dans les chantiers, ah! n'hivernerons
    plus!
    Dans les chantiers, ah! n'hivernerons
    plus!

5. Then your family with great joy
   Welcome home their shanty boy.
   Father greets you at the gate,
   Mother piles food on your plate.

6. When they welcome you with cheer
   You will say both loud and clear:
   'To the devil with the shack!
   Never more will I go back!'

FINAL CHORUS:
    No more we'll go to the winter camp!
    No more we'll go to the winter camp!

24. THE JONES BOYS

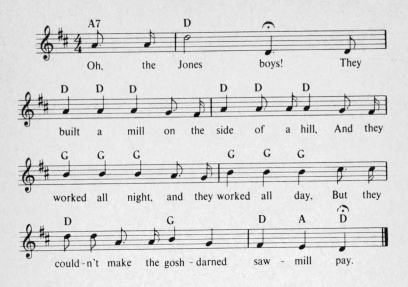

Oh, the Jones boys! They
built a mill on the side of a hill, And they
worked all night, and they worked all day, But they
could-n't make the gosh - darned saw - mill pay.

Oh, the Jones boys!
They built a mill on the side of a hill,
And they worked all night, and they worked all day,
But they couldn't make the gosh-darned saw-mill pay.

25. JIMMY WHELAN

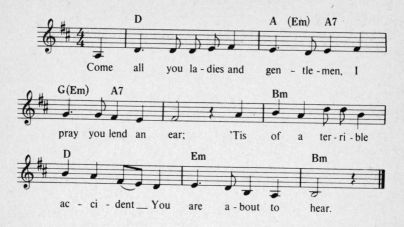

Come all you la-dies and gen-tle-men, I pray you lend an ear; 'Tis of a ter-ri-ble ac-ci-dent__ You are a-bout to hear.

1. Come all you ladies and gentlemen,
   I pray you lend an ear;
   'Tis of a terrible accident
   You are about to hear.

2. 'Tis of a young and active youth,
   Jimmy Whelan he was called;
   He was drownded on McClellan's
      drive
   All on the Upper Falls.

3. The fierce and the raging main,
   The waters they ran high,
   And the foreman said to Whelan:
   'This jam you will have to try.

4. 'You've always been an active youth
   While danger's lurking near,
   So you are the man I want to help
   To keep these waters clear.'

5. Whelan he made answer
   Unto his comrades bold:
   'Supposing if there's danger
   We will do as we are told.

6. 'We'll obey our foreman's orders
   As noble men should do.'
   Just as he spoke the jam it broke
   And let poor Whelan through.

7. The raging main it tossed and tore
   Those logs from shore to shore,
   And here and there his body went,
   A-tumbling o'er and o'er.

8. No earthly man could ever live
   In such a raging main.
   Poor Whelan struggled hard for life
   But he struggled all in vain.

9. There were three of them in danger,
   But two of them were saved.
   It was noble-hearted Whelan
   That met with a watery grave.

10. So come all you young and active
      youths,
    A warning from me take,
    And try and shun all danger
    Before it gets too late,

11. For death is drawing nearer
    And trying to destroy
    The pride of some poor mother's
      heart,
    And his father's only joy.

69

26. LOST JIMMY WHELAN

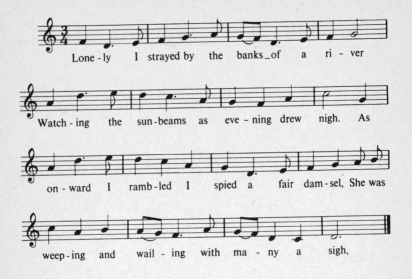

Lone-ly I strayed by the banks _ of a ri – ver
Watch – ing the sun - beams as eve – ning drew nigh. As
on - ward I ramb-led I spied a fair dam - sel, She was
weep - ing and wail – ing with ma – ny a sigh,

1. Lonely I strayed by the banks of a river
   Watching the sunbeams as evening drew nigh.
   As onward I rambled I spied a fair damsel,
   She was weeping and wailing with many a sigh,

2. Crying for one who is now lying lonely,
   Sighing for one who no mortal could see,
   For the dark rolling waters flow gently around him
   As onwards she speeds over young Jimmy's grave.

3. She cries, 'O my darling won't you come to my arrums
   And give me fond kisses which ofttimes you gave?
   You promised to meet me this evening, my darling,
   So now, lovelie Jimmy, arise from your grave.'

4. Slowly he rose from the dark stormy waters,
   A vision of beauty far fairer than sun.
   Pink and red were the garments all round him,
   And unto this fair maid to speak he began,

5. Saying, 'Why do you rise me from the re-alms of glory
   Back to this place where I once had to leave?'
   'It was to embrace in your strong loving arrums,
   So now lovelie Jimmy, take me to your grave.'

6. 'Darling,' he says, 'you are asking a favour
   That no earthly mortal could grant unto thee,
   For death is the debtor that tore us asunder,
   And wide is the gulf, love, between you and me.

7. 'Hard, hard were the struggles on the cruel Mississippi,
   But encircled around her on every side,
   Thinking of you as we conquered them bravely,
   I was hoping some day for to make you my bride.

8. 'But in vain was the hopes that arose in my bosom,
   And nothing, oh nothing, on earth could be saved.
   My last dying thoughts were of God and you, darling,
   Till death took me down to the deep silent grave.

9. 'One fond embrace, love, and then I must leave you.
   One loving farewell, and then we must part.'
   Cold were the arms that encircled around her,
   And cold was the form that she pressed to her heart.

10. Slowly he rose from the banks of the river,
    Up to the sky he then seemed to go,
    Leaving this fair maid on the banks of the river,
    Sighing and weeping in anger and woe.

11. Throwing herself on the banks of the river,
    Crying as though her poor heart it would break,
    She cried, 'O my darling, my lost Jimmy Whelan,
    I'll lie down and die by the side of your grave.'

27. PETER EMBERLEY

My name 'tis Peter Em-ber-ley, as you may un-der-stand. I was born on Prince Ed-ward's Is-land near by the o-cean strand. In eigh-teen hun-dred and eigh-ty-four when the flo-wers were a bril-liant hue, I left my na-tive coun-ter-ie____ my for-tune to pur-sue.

1. My name 'tis Peter Emberley, as you may understand.
   I was born on Prince Edward's Island near by the ocean strand.
   In eighteen hundred and eighty-four when the flowers were a brilliant hue,
   I left my native counterie my fortune to pursue.

2. I landed in New Brunswick in a lumbering counterie,
   I hired to work in the lumber woods on the Sou-West Miramichi.
   I hired to work in the lumber woods where they cut the tall spruce down,
   While loading teams with yarded logs I received a deadly wound.

3. There's danger on the ocean where the waves roll mountains high,
   There's danger on the battlefield where the angry bullets fly,
   There's danger in the lumber woods, for death lurks sullen there,
   And I have fell a victim into that monstrous snare.

4. I know my luck seems very hard since fate has proved severe,
   But victor death is the worst can come and I have no more to fear.
   And he'll allay those deadly pains and liberate me soon,
   And I'll sleep the long and lonely sleep called slumber in the tomb.

5. Here's adieu to Prince Edward's Island, that garden in the seas,
   No more I'll walk its flowery banks to enjoy a summer's breeze.
   No more I'll view those gallant ships as they go swimming by
   With their streamers floating on the breeze above the canvas high.

6. Here's adieu unto my father, it was him who drove me here,
   I thought he used me cruelly, his treatments were unfair,
   For 'tis not right to oppress a boy or try to keep him down,
   'Twill oft repulse him from his home when he is far too young.

7. Here's adieu unto my greatest friend, I mean my mother dear,
   She raised a son who fell as soon as he left her tender care.
   'Twas little did my mother know when she sang lullaby,
   What country I might travel in or what death I might die.

8. Here's adieu unto my youngest friend, those island girls so true,
   Long may they bloom to grace that isle where first my breath I drew.
   For the world will roll on just the same when I have passed away,
   What signifies a mortal man whose origin is clay?

9. But there's a world beyond the tomb, to it I'm nearing on,
   Where man is more than mortal and death can never come.
   The mist of death it glares my eyes and I'm no longer here,
   My spirit takes its final flight unto another sphere.

10. (And now before I pass away there is one more thing I crave,
    That some good holy father will bless my mouldering grave,
    Near by the city of Boiestown where my mouldering bones do lay,
    A-waiting for my Saviour's call on that great Judgement Day.)

28. WHEN THE SHANTYBOY COMES DOWN

1. When the shantyboy comes down, in his pockets fifty pound,
   He will look around some pretty girl to find.
   If he finds her not too shy, with a dark and rolling eye,
   The poor shantyboy is well pleased in his mind.

2. When the landlady comes in, she is neat and very trim;
   She is like an evening star.
   If she finds him in good trim, she is always ready to wait on him,
   And from one to two they'll sit up on the bar.

3. So the shantyboy goes on till his money is all gone
   And the landlady begins for to fret.
   So he says, 'My lady, do not fret, I will pay my honest debt,
   And bid adieu to the girl I had in town.

4. 'There's a gang in command, so the old folks understand,
   And it's for the backwoods they are bound.
   With a whisky and a song we will shove our old canoe along,
   Bid adieu to the girl I had in town.'

IV. THE LAND

29. THE SCARBOROUGH SETTLER'S LAMENT

1. Away wi' Canada's muddy creeks and Canada's fields of pine!
   Your land of wheat is a goodly land, but ah! it isna mine!
   The heathy hill, the grassy dale, the daisy-spangled lea,
   The purling burn and craggy linn, auld Scotia's glens, gie me.

2. Oh, I wad like to hear again the lark on Tinny's hill,
   And see the wee bit gowany that blooms beside the rill.
   Like banished Swiss who views afar his Alps wi' longing e'e,
   I gaze upon the morning star that shines on my countrie.

3. Nae mair I'll win by Eskdale Pen, or Pentland's craggy cone;
   The days can ne'er come back again of thirty years that's gone;
   But fancy oft at midnight hour will steal across the sea:
   Yestreen amid a pleasant dream I saw the auld countrie.

4. Each well known scene that met my view brought childhood's joys to mind,
   The blackbird sang on Tushy linn the song he sang lang syne,
   But like a dream time flies away, again the morning came,
   And I awoke in Canada, three thousand miles 'frae hame'.

30. THE BACKWOODSMAN

Oh, it's well do I re-mem-ber the year of 'for-ty - five, I think my-self quite hap - py to find my-self a - live. I har - nessed up my hor - ses, my busi - ness to pur - sue, And I went a - haul - ing cord - wood as I of - ten used to do.

1. Oh, it's well do I remember the year of 'forty-five,
   I think myself quite happy to find myself alive.
   I harnessed up my horses, my business to pursue,
   And I went a-hauling cordwood as I often used to do.

2. Now I only hauled one load where I should have hauled four.
   I went down to Omemee and I could not haul no more.
   The taverns they being open, good liquor was flowing free,
   And I hadn't emptied one glass when another was filled for me.

3. Now I met with an old acquaintance, and I dare not tell his name.
   He was going to a dance and I thought I'd do the same.
   He was going to a dance where the fiddle was sweetly played,
   And the boys and girls all danced till the breaking of the day.

4. So I puts me saddle on me arm and started for the barn
   To saddle up old gray nag, not thinking any harm.
   I saddled up old gray nag, and I rode away so still,
   And I never drew a long breath till I came to Downeyville.

5. So when I got to Downeyville the night was far advanced.
   I got upon the floor for to have a little dance.
   The fiddler he being rested, his arm being stout and strong,
   Played the rounds of old Ireland for four hours long.

6. Now my father followed after, I've heard the people say;
   He must have had a pilot or he never would found the way.
   He looked in every keyhole that he could see a light
   Till his old gray locks were wet *with the dew of the night*.

31. THE HONEST WORKING MAN

'Way down in East Cape Bre - ton, where they knit the sock and mit - ten, Chez - zet - cook is rep - re - sent - ed by the hus - ky black and tan. May they ne - ver be re - ject - ed, and home rule be pro - tect - ed And al - ways be con - nect - ed with the ho - nest work - ing man.

CHORUS:

'Way down in East Cape Breton, where they knit the sock and mitten,
Chezzetcook is represented by the husky black and tan.
May they never be rejected, and home rule be protected
And always be connected with the honest working man.

1. What raises high my dander, next door lives a Newfoundlander,
   Whose wife you cannot stand her, since high living she began,
   Along with the railroad rackers, also the codfish packers,
   Who steal the cheese and crackers from the honest working man.

2. When leaves fall in the autumn and fish freeze to the bottom,
   They take a three-ton schooner and go round the western shore;
   They load her with provisions, hard tack and codfish mizzens,
   The like I never heard of since the downfall of Bras d'Or.

3. The man who mixes mortar gets a dollar and a quarter,
   The sugar-factory worker, he gets a dollar ten,
   While there's my next-door neighbour, who subsists on outside labour,
   In the winter scarcely earns enough to feed a sickly hen.

4. They cross the Bay of Fundy, they reach her on a Monday:
   Did you see my brother Angus? Now tell me if you can.
   He was once a soap-box greaseman, but now he is a policeman,
   Because he could not earn a living as an honest working man.

32. L'HABITANT D'SAINT-BARBE

1. L'habitant d'Saint-Barb' s'en va t'à Montréal,
   L'habitant d'Saint-Barb' s'en va t'à Montréal.

2. La femm' d'l'habitant d'Saint-Barb' s'en va t'à Montréal,
   La femm' d'l'habitant d'Saint-Barb' s'en va t'à Montréal.

3. L'enfant d'la femm' d'l'habitant d'Saint-Barb' s'en va t'à Montréal,
   L'enfant d'la femm' d'l'habitant d'Saint-Barb' s'en va t'à Montréal.

4. Le chien d'l'enfant d'la femm' d'l'habitant de Saint-Barb' . . .

5. La queue du chien d'l'enfant d'la femm' d'l'habitant de Saint-Barb' . . .

6. Le bout d'la queue du chien d'l'enfant d'la femm' d'l'habitant de Saint-Barb' . . .

33. LIFE IN A PRAIRIE SHACK

Oh, a life in a prai - rie shack,___ when the rain be - gins to pour!___ Drip, drip, it comes through the roof,___ and some comes through the door.___ The ten-der-foot cur -ses his fate___ and faint - ly mut -ters, 'Ah!___ This bloom - ing coun-try's a fraud,___ and I want to go home to my Maw!'___ 'Maw!___ Maw!___ I want to go home to my Maw!___ This bloom - ing coun - try's a fraud___ and I want to go home to my Maw!'___

1. Oh, a life in a prairie shack, when the rain begins to pour!
   Drip, drip, it comes through the roof, and some comes through the door.
   The tenderfoot curses his fate and faintly mutters, 'Ah!
   This blooming country's a fraud, and I want to go home to my Maw!'

CHORUS:
   'Maw! Maw! I want to go home to my Maw!
   This blooming country's a fraud, and I want to go home to my Maw!'

2. Oh, he saddled his fiery cayuse, determined to flourish around;
   The critter began to buck, and threw him off on the ground,
   And as he picked himself up he was heard to mutter, 'Ah!
   This blooming country's a fraud, and I want to go home to my Maw!'

3. Oh, he tried to light a fire at twenty degrees below.
   He made a lick at a stick and amputated his toe,
   And as he crawled to his shack he was heard to mutter, 'Ah!
   This blooming country's a fraud, and I want to go home to my Maw!'

4. Now all you tenderfeet list, before you go too far:
   If you haven't a government sit, you'd better stay where you are,
   And if you take my advice, then you will not mutter, 'Ah!
   This blooming country's a fraud, and I want to go home to my Maw!'

34. THE ALBERTA HOMESTEADER

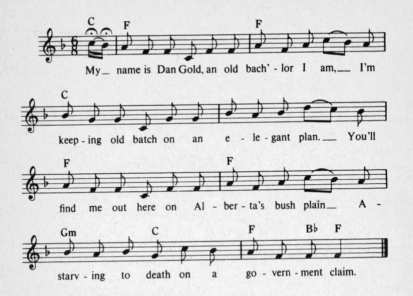

My name is Dan Gold, an old bach'-lor I am,— I'm keep-ing old batch on an e-le-gant plan.— You'll find me out here on Al-ber-ta's bush plain— A-starv-ing to death on a go-vern-ment claim.

1. My name is Dan Gold, an old bach'lor I am,
   I'm keeping old batch on an elegant plan.
   You'll find me out here on Alberta's bush plain
   A-starving to death on a government claim.

2. So come to Alberta, there's room for you all,
   Where the wind never ceases and the rain always falls,
   Where the sun always sets and there it remains
   Till we get frozen out on our government claims.

3. My house it is built of the natural soil,
   My walls are erected according to Hoyle,
   My roof has no pitch, it is level and plain,
   And I always get wet when it happens to rain.

4. My clothes are all ragged, my language is rough,
   My bread is case-hardened and solid and tough,
   My dishes are scattered all over the room,
   My floor gets afraid at the sight of a broom.

5. How happy I feel when I roll into bed:
   The rattlesnake rattles a tune at my head,
   The little mosquito devoid of all fear
   Crawls over my face and into my ear.

6. The little bedbug so cheerful and bright,
   It keeps me up laughing two-thirds of the night,
   And the smart little flea with tacks in his toes
   Crawls up through my whiskers and tickles my nose.

7. You may try to raise wheat, you may try to raise rye,
   You may stay there and live, you may stay there and die,
   But as for myself, I'll no longer remain
   A-starving to death on a government claim.

8. So farewell to Alberta, farewell to the west,
   It's backwards I'll go to the girl I love best.
   I'll go back to the east and get me a wife
   And never eat cornbread the rest of my life.

V. SOCIAL LIFE

35. THE KELLIGREWS SOIREE

You may talk of Cla - ra No - lan's ball or a - ny-thing you choose, But it could - n't hold a snuff - box to the spree at Kel - li - grews. If you want your eye - balls straight-ened just come out next week with me And you'll have to wear your glas - ses at the Kel - li-grews Soi - ree. There was birch rine, tar twine, cher - ry wine and tur - pen -tine, Jowls and ca - va - lan - ces, gin - ger beer and tea, Pigs' feet, cat's meat, dump - lings boiled in a sheet, Dan - de - lion and

90

cra - ckies' teeth at the Kel - li - grews Soi - ree.____

1. You may talk of Clara Nolan's ball or anything you choose,
   But it couldn't hold a snuff-box to the spree at Kelligrews.
   If you want your eye-balls straightened just come out next week with me
   And you'll have to wear your glasses at the Kelligrews Soiree.
       There was birch rine, tar twine, cherry wine and turpentine,
       Jowls and cavalances, ginger beer and tea,
       Pigs' feet, cats' meat, dumplings boiled in a sheet,
       Dandelion and crackies' teeth at the Kelligrews Soiree.

2. Oh, I borrowed Cluney's beaver as I squared my yards to sail,
   And a swallow-tail from Hogan that was foxy on the tail,
   Billy Cuddahy's old working pants and Patsy Nolan's shoes,
   And an old white vest from Fogarty to sport at Kelligrews.
       There was Dan Milley, Joe Lilly, Tantan and Mrs Tilley
       Dancing like a little filly; 'twould raise your heart to see.
       Jim Bryan, Din Ryan, Flipper Smith and Caroline –
       I tell you boys we had a time at the Kelligrews Soiree.

3. Oh, when I arrived at Betsey Snooks' that night at half past eight,
   The place was blocked with carriages stood waiting at the gate.
   With Cluney's funnel on my pate, the first words Betsey said:
   'Here comes a local preacher with the pulpit on his head.'
       There was Bill Mews, Dan Hughes, Wilson, Taft and Teddy Roose,
       While Bryant he sat in the blues and looking hard at me;
       Jim Fling, Tom King and Johnson, champion of the ring,
       And all the boxers I could bring at the Kelligrews Soiree.

4. The Saratoga Lancers first, Miss Betsey kindly said;
   Sure I danced with Nancy Cronan and her Grannie on the 'Head';
   And Hogan danced with Betsey: oh, you should have seen his shoes
   As he lashed old muskets from the rack that night at Kelligrews.
       There was boiled guineas, cold guineas, bullocks' heads and picaninies
       And everything to catch the pennies, you'd break your sides to see.
       Boiled duff, cold duff, apple jam was in a cuff,
       I tell you boys, we had enough at the Kelligrews Soiree.

5. Crooked Flavin struck the fiddler and a hand I then took in;
   You should see George Cluney's beaver, and it flattened to the rim!
   And Hogan's coat was like a vest – the tails were gone you see.
   Oh, says I, 'The devil haul ye and your Kelligrews Soiree.'

91

36. BACHELOR'S HALL

1. Oh, the girls of this place that live along the shore,
   If they hear but one word they will speak it twice o'er;
   And then they'll add to it as much as they can,
   But the fairest of women look out for a man,

CHORUS:
   And it's oh – – – – – oh – oh – oh laddie – oh.

2. The boys that dress up in the very best style
   To court the young girls sure it is their incline;
   They'll go to their houses and there they will stay,
   And they'll keep the girls up till it's almost day . . .

3. The girls go to bed and sleep all the next day;
   Their mothers get up, there's the devil to pay:
   'O mother, dear mother, sure I'm not to blame,
   For when you were young you were fond of the same,' . . .

4. The boys they get up and they stagger and reel,
   They curse on the girls how unsteady they feel:
   'If this what's called courting I'll court none at all;
   I'll live by myself and keep Bachelor's Hall,' . . .

5. Oh Bachelor's Hall it is always the best:
   Be you sick, drunk or sober you are always at rest;
   Come in when you like and lie down on the straw,
   You can eat the whole cake be it done or be it raw . . .

6. Oh, Bachelor's Hall it is always the best,
   Be you sick, drunk or sober you are always at rest;
   No wife for to scold you, no children to bawl;
   Oh, happy's the man that keeps Bachelor's Hall . . .

7. And now my little song it is nearly done,
   I hope that I have not offended anyone;
   If there's anyone here who takes any offence,
   They can go to the devil and seek recompense! . . .

37. FELLER FROM FORTUNE

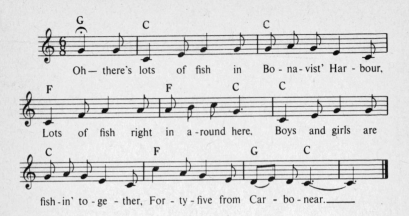

Oh — there's lots of fish in Bo - na - vist' Har - bour, Lots of fish right in a -round here. Boys and girls are fish -in' to - ge - ther, For - ty - five from Car - bo - near.

1. Oh – there's lots of fish in Bonavist' Harbour,
   Lots of fish right in around here,
   Boys and girls are fishin' together,
   Forty-five from Carbonear.

CHORUS:
   Oh – catch a-hold this one, catch a-hold that one,
   Swing around this one, swing around she.
   Dance around this one, dance around that one,
   Diddle-dum this one, diddle-dum dee.

2. Oh – Sally is the pride of Cat Harbour,
   Ain't been swung since last year,
   Drinkin' rum and wine and cassis
   What the boys brought home from St Pierre.

3. Oh – Sally goes to church every Sunday
   Not for to sing nor for to hear,
   But to see the feller from Fortune
   What was down here fishin' the year.

4. Oh – Sally's got a bouncin' new baby,
   Father said that he didn't care,
   'Cause she got that from the feller from Fortune
   What was down here fishin' the year.

5. Oh – Uncle George got up in the mornin',
   He got up in an 'ell of a tear,
   And he ripped the arse right out of his britches,
   Now he's got ne'er pair to wear.

6. Oh – there's lots of fish in Bonavist' Harbour,
   Lots of fishermen in around here;
   Swing your partner, Jimmy Joe Jacobs –
   I'll be home in the spring of the year.

38. DUFFY'S HOTEL

1. If you're longing for fun and enjoyment, or inclined to go out on a spree,
   Come along with me over to Boiestown on the banks of the Miramichi.
   You'll meet with a royal reception; my 'ventures to you I'll relate;
   On the eighteenth of May I arrived here, from Fred'ricton – came on the
      freight.

2. One night I went out on a party; I tell you 'twas something immense,
    We collared a Shanghai rooster, and he just cost us seventeen cents.
    He was sick with the croup and the measles; they said he was too poor to sell,
    But I guess he made hash for the boarders that put up at Duffy's Hotel.

3. One night I went out on a party along with the rest of the boys.
    We got full of peely island; I tell you we made lots of noise.
    We frightened the pigs up in Tugtown; caused the Pleasant Ridge dogs for to
        yell
    And when we got kicked out of Hayesville, we struck 'er for Duffy's Hotel.

4. One night I went out on a party; 'twas held in the Mansion below.
    A row was kicked up in the kitchen; I tell you it wasn't too slow.
    We upset the chairs and the tables; the windows and stove, too, they fell.
    This row was kicked up by Delaney, a boarder at Duffy's Hotel.

5. Well, friends, I must bid you good evening for fear you will think me a Turk.
    If I linger round here any longer some fellows might give me a jerk!
    I'll go back to the scenes of my childhood, in peace and contentment to dwell;
    Bid adieu to the kind entertainment I met with at Duffy's Hotel.

39. ALOUETTE

A - lou - et - te, gen - tille a - lou - et - te,
a - lou - et - te, je t'y plu - me - rai.
A - lou - et - te, gen - tille a - lou - et - te,
a - lou - et - te, je t'y plu - me - rai.
Je t'y plu - me - rai la têt', je t'y
plu - me - rai la têt', Je t'y plu - me - rai la têt', je t'y
plu - me - rai la têt', Et la têt', Et la têt',
A - lou - ett', A - lou - ett', O!

Alouette, gentille alouette, alouette, je t'y plumerai.
Alouette, gentille alouette, alouette, je t'y plumerai.

1. Je t'y plumerai la têt', je t'y plumerai la têt',
   Je t'y plumerai la têt', je t'y plumerai la têt',
   Et la têt', ⎱
   Et la têt', ⎰ 2
   Alouett',
   Alouett', O . . .

2. Je t'y plumerai le bec, je t'y plumerai le bec,
   Je t'y plumerai le bec, je t'y plumerai le bec,

   Et le bec, ⎱
   Et le bec, ⎰ 2
   Et la têt', ⎱
   Et la têt', ⎰ 2

   Alouett',
   Alouett', O . . .

(Continue adding a different part of the bird's body in each verse:
le nez, les yeux, le cou, les ail's, le dos, les patt's, la queue . . .)

40. AH! SI MON MOINE VOULAIT DANSER!

English words by Edith Fowke

Ah! si mon moi - ne vou - lait dan - ser! Ah!
si mon moi - ne vou - lait dan - ser! Un
ca - pu - chon je lui don - ne - rais, Un
ca - pu - chon je lui don - ne - rais. Dan - se, mon moin',
dan - se! Tu n'en - tends pas la dan - se, Tu
n'en - tends pas mon mou - lin, lon la, Tu
n'en - tends pas mon mou - lin mar - cher.

1. Ah! si mon moine voulait danser!
   Ah! si mon moine voulait danser!
   Un capuchon je lui donnerais,
   Un capuchon je lui donnerais.

REFRAIN:
   Danse, mon moin', danse!
   Tu n'entends pas la danse,
   Tu n'entends pas mon moulin, lon la,
   Tu n'entends pas mon moulin marcher.

1. If you will come and dance with me,
   If you will come and dance with me,
   A feathered cap I will give to thee,
   A feathered cap I will give to thee.

CHORUS:
   Come, my lass, let's trip now!
   Together let us skip now!
   As lightly on the measures go,
   Our feet move merrily to and fro.

2. Ah! si mon moine voulait danser!)2
   Un ceinturon je lui donnerais.)2

3. Ah! si mon moine voulait danser!)2
   Un chapelet je lui donnerais.)2

4. Ah! si mon moine voulait danser!)2
   Un froc de bur' je lui donnerais.)2

5. Ah! si mon moine voulait danser!)2
   Un beau psautier je lui donnerais.)2

6. S'il n'avait fait vœu de pauvreté)2
   Bien d'autres choses je lui
   donnerais.)2

2. If you will come and dance with
   me,)2
   Bright silver shoes I will give to
   thee.)2

3. If you will come and dance with
   me,)2
   A dress of blue I will give to thee.)2

4. If you will come and dance with
   me,)2
   A kiss or two I will give to thee.)2

5. And if you'll give me a kiss or two,)2
   A ring of gold I will give to you.)2

41. EN ROULANT MA BOULE

English words by Edith Fowke

En rou-lant ma bou-le rou-lant, En rou-lant ma bou - le.

Der - rièr' chez nous ya t'un é - tang, En rou - lant ma

bou - le. Der - rièr' chez nous ya t'un é - tang,

En rou - lant ma bou - le. Trois beaux ca - nards s'en

vont bai - gnant, Rou - li, rou - lant, ma bou - le rou - lant.

REFRAIN:
En roulant ma boule roulant, or V'là l'bon vent...
En roulant ma boule.
En roulant ma boule roulant,
En roulant ma boule.

1. Derrièr' chez nous ya t'un étang,
   En roulant ma boule.
   Derrièr' chez nous ya t'un étang,
   En roulant ma boule.
   Trois beaux canards s'en vont
   baignant,
   Rouli, roulant, ma boule roulant.

1. Behind our house we have a pond,
   En roulant ma boule.
   Behind our house we have a pond,
   En roulant ma boule.
   Behind our house we have a pond
   Where three fine ducks swim round
   and round.

2. Trois beaux canards s'en vont
   baignant...
   Le fils du roi s'en va chassant.

2. To hunt them comes the young king's
   son...
   With him he brings his shining gun.

3. Le fils du roi s'en va chassant...
   Avec son grand fusil d'argent.

3. He aims it at the black for fun...
   But then he hits the whitest one.

102

4. Avec son grand fusil d'argent . . .
   Visa le noir, tua le blanc.

5. Visa le noir, tua le blanc . . .
   Ô fils du roi, tu es méchant!

6. Ô fils du roi, tu es méchant! . . .
   D'avoir tué mon canard blanc.

7. D'avoir tué mon canard blanc . . .
   Par dessous l'aile il perd son sang.

8. Par dessous l'aile il perd son sang . . .
   Par les yeux lui sort'nt des diamants.

9. Par les yeux lui sort'nt des
   diamants . . .
   Et par le bec l'or et l'argent.

10. Et par le bec l'or et l'argent . . .
    Toutes ses plum's s'en vont au vent.

11. Toutes ses plum's s'en vont au
    vent . . .
    Trois dam's s'en vont les ramassant.

12. Trois dam's s'en vont les
    ramassant . . .
    C'est pour en faire un lit de camp.

13. C'est pour en faire un lit de camp . . .
    Pour y coucher tous les passants.

4. 'O prince, now see what you have
   done! . . .
   You've killed my duck, the whitest
   one!'

5. From his bright eyes two diamonds
   fall . . .
   And from his bill drops gold for all.

6. Out from his wing the red drops
   pour . . .
   And on the wind his feathers soar.

7. Three maidens fair his feathers
   take . . .
   A bed for weary men to make.

42. D'OÙ VIENS-TU, BERGÈRE?

English words by Edith Fowke

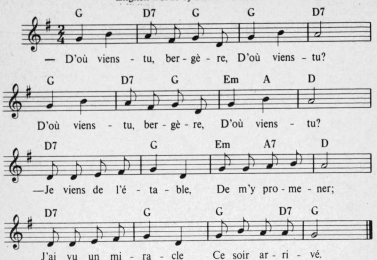

— D'où viens - tu, ber - gè - re, D'où viens - tu?

D'où viens - tu, ber - gè - re, D'où viens - tu?

—Je viens de l'é - ta - ble, De m'y pro - me - ner;

J'ai vu un mi - ra - cle Ce soir ar - ri - vé.

1. – D'où viens-tu, bergère,
    D'où viens-tu? } 2
– Je viens de l'étable,
De m'y promener;
J'ai vu un miracle
Ce soir arrivé.

2. – Qu' as-tu vu, bergère,
    Qu'as-tu vu? } 2
– J'ai vu dans la crèche
Un petit enfant
Sur la paille fraîche
Mis bien tendrement.

3. – Rien de plus, bergère,
    Rien de plus? } 2
– Saint' Marie, sa mère,
Qui lui fait boir' du lait,
Saint Joseph, son père,
Qui tremble de froid.

1. 'Whence, O shepherd maiden,
    Whence come you?' } 2
'I come from the stable
Where this very night
My eyes have been dazzled
By a wondrous sight.'

2. 'What saw you, O maiden,
    What saw you?' } 2
'Right there in the manger
A little child I saw.
Softly he lay sleeping
On the yellow straw.'

3. 'Nothing more, O maiden,
    Nothing more?' } 2
'There his mother Mary
Did her babe enfold,
While his father Joseph
Trembled with the cold.'

4. – Rien de plus, bergère, }2
     Rien de plus ?
   – Y a le bœuf et l'âne
   Qui sont par devant,
   Avec leur haleine
   Réchauffent l'enfant.

5. – Rien de plus, bergère, }2
     Rien de plus ?
   – Y a trois petits anges
   Descendus du ciel
   Chantant les louanges
   Du Père éternel.

4. 'Nothing more, O maiden, }2
     Nothing more ?'
   'Ox and ass before him
   Paid their homage mild ;
   With their gentle breathing
   Warmed the Holy Child.'

5. 'Nothing more, O maiden, }2
     Nothing more ?'
   'Then came three bright angels
   From the starry sky,
   Singing forth their praises
   To the Lord on high.'

43. I'SE THE B'Y THAT BUILDS THE BOAT

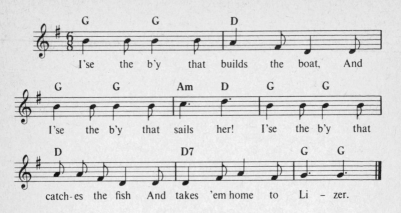

1. I'se the b'y that builds the boat,
   And I'se the b'y that sails her!
   I'se the b'y that catches the fish
   And takes 'em home to Lizer.

   CHORUS:
   Hip yer partner, Sally Tibbo!
   Hip yer partner, Sally Brown!
   Fogo, Twillingate, Mor'ton's
   Harbour,
   All around the circle!

2. Sods and rinds to cover yer flake,
   Cake and tea for supper,
   Codfish in the spring o' the year
   Fried in maggoty butter.

3. I don't want your maggoty fish,
   That's no good for winter;
   I could buy as good as that
   Down in Bonavister.

4. I took Lizer to a dance
   And faith but she could travel!
   And every step that she did take
   Was up to her knees in gravel.

5. Susan White, she's out of sight,
   Her petticoat wants a border;
   Old Sam Oliver, in the dark,
   He kissed her in the corner.

106

44. WHO'LL BE KING BUT CHARLIE?

Come ___ round the hea-ther, Come o'er the hea-ther, You're wel - come late and ear - ly. A - round him fling your roy - al king, For who'll be king ___ but Char - lie? Char - lie likes to kiss the girls, Char - lie likes the bran - dy, Char - lie likes to kiss the girls When-e - ver they ___ come han - dy. *Come* (to CHORUS)

CHORUS:
Come round the heather,
Come o'er the heather,
You're welcome late and early.
Around him fling your royal king,
For who'll be king but Charlie?

Charlie likes to kiss the girls,
Charlie likes the brandy,
Charlie likes to kiss the girls
Whenever they come handy.

VI. TRUE LOVERS

45. VIVE LA CANADIENNE!

English words by Edith Fowke

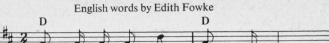

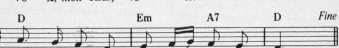

1. Vive la Canadienne!
   Vole, mon cœur, vole!
   Vive la Canadienne
   Et ses jolis yeux doux,
   Et ses jolis yeux doux, doux,
      doux,
   Et ses jolis yeux doux.
   ⎬2

1. Of my Canadian girl I sing,
   Gaily our voices ring!
   Of my Canadian girl I sing
   And her sweet eyes so blue,
   And her sweet eyes so blue,
      blue, blue,
   And her sweet eyes so blue.
   ⎬2

110

2. Nous la menons aux noces,
   Vole, mon cœur, vole!
   Nous la menons aux noces
   Dans tous ses beaux atours,
   Dans tous ses beaux atours,
     'tours, 'tours,   } 2
   Dans tous ses beaux atours.

3. On danse avec nos blondes,
   Vole, mon cœur, vole!
   On danse avec nos blondes;
   Nous changeons tour à tour,
   Nous changeons tour à tour,
     tour, tour,   } 2
   Nous changeons tour à tour.

4. Ainsi le temps se passe,
   Vole, mon cœur, vole!
   Ainsi le temps se passe:
   Il est vraiment bien doux!
   Il est vraiment bien doux,
     doux, doux,   } 2
   Il est vraiment bien doux!

2. Here's to a lovers' meeting!
   Gaily our voices ring!
   Here's to a lovers' meeting!
   I know that she is true,
   I know that she is true, true,
     true,   } 2
   I know that she is true.

3. Quickly our hearts are beating!
   Gaily our voices ring!
   Quickly our hearts are beating,
   As we go on our way,
   As we go on our way, way,
     way,   } 2
   As we go on our way.

4. So go the hours a-flying,
   Gaily our voices ring!
   So go the hours a-flying
   Until our wedding day,
   Until our wedding day, day,
     day,   } 2
   Until our wedding day.

46. THE STAR OF BELLE ISLE

One eve-ning for plea-sure I ramb-led ___ To ___ view the fair fields all a - lone. ___ It was down by the banks of Loch E - rin ___ Where ___ beau - ty and ___ plea - sure were known.

1. One evening for pleasure I rambled
   To view the fair fields all alone.
   It was down by the banks of Loch Erin
   Where beauty and pleasure were known.

2. I spied a fair maid at her labour,
   Which caused me to stay for awhile;
   I thought her the goddess of beauty,
   The blooming bright star of Belle Isle.

3. I humbled myself to her beauty:
   'Fair maiden, where do you belong?
   Are you from the heavens descended,
   Abiding in Cupid's fair throng?'

4. 'Young man, I will tell you a secret,
   It's true I'm a maid that is poor,
   And to part with my vows and my promises,
   'Tis more than my poor heart can endure.

5. 'Therefore I'll remain at my service,
   And go through all hardship and toil,
   And wait for the lad that do love me,
   Alone on the banks of Belle Isle.'

6. 'Young maiden, I wish not to banter,
   It's true I came here in disguise;
   I came to fulfil my last promise,
   And hoped to give you a surprise.

7. 'I own you're the maid I love dearly,
   You've been in my heart all the while;
   For there's no other damsel in this wide world
   Than my blooming bright star of Belle Isle.'

47. THE STAR OF LOGY BAY

Ye ladies and ye gentlemen, I pray you lend an ear, While I locate the residence of a lovely charmer fair. The curling of her yellow locks first stole my heart away, And her place of habitation is down in Logy Bay.

1. Ye ladies and ye gentlemen, I pray you lend an ear,
   While I locate the residence of a lovely charmer fair.
   The curling of her yellow locks first stole my heart away,
   And her place of habitation is down in Logy Bay.

2. It was on a summer's evening this little place I found.
   I met her agéd father who did me sore confound,
   Saying: 'If you address my daughter I'll send her far away,
   And she never will return again while you're in Logy Bay.'

3. How could you be so cruel as to part me from my love?
   Her tender heart beats in her breast as constant as a dove.
   Oh, Venus was no fairer, nor the lovely month of May.
   May heaven above shower down its love on the star of Logy Bay.

4. 'Twas on the very next morning he went to St John's town
   And engaged for her a passage in a vessel outward bound.
   He robbed me of my heart's delight and sent her far away,
   And he left me here downhearted for the star of Logy Bay.

5. Oh, now I'll go a-roaming, I can no longer stay,
   I'll search the wide world over in every counterie –
   I'll search in vain through France and Spain, likewise Americay,
   'Till I will sight my heart's delight, the star of Logy Bay.

6. Now to conclude and finish, the truth to you I'll tell.
   Between Torbay and Outer Cove, 'tis there my love did dwell:
   The finest girl that graced our Isle, so every one did say.
   May heaven above send down its love on the star of Logy Bay!

48. MARY ANN

Oh, fare thee well, my own true love! Fare thee well, my dear! _____ For the ship is ____ wait - ing, the wind blows high, And I am bound a - way for the sea, Ma - ry Ann! ____ And I am bound a - way for the sea, Ma - ry Ann!

1. Oh, fare thee well, my own true love!
   Fare thee well, my dear!
   For the ship is waiting, the wind blows high,
   And I am bound away for the sea, Mary Ann!
   And I am bound away for the sea, Mary Ann!

2. Oh, yonder don't you see the dove
   Sitting on the stile?
   She's mourning the loss of her own true love,
   As I do now for you, my sweetheart, Mary Ann!
   As I do now for you, my sweetheart, Mary Ann!

3. A lobster boiling in the pot,
   A blue fish in the brook,
   They are suffering long, but it's nothing like
   The ache I bear for you, my sweetheart, Mary Ann!
   The ache I bear for you, my sweetheart, Mary Ann!

116

4. Oh, had I but a flask of gin,
   Sugar here for two,
   And a great big bowl for to mix it in,
   I'd pour a drink for you, my sweetheart, Mary Ann!
   I'd pour a drink for you, my sweetheart, Mary Ann!

49. C'EST L'AVIRON

English words by Edith Fowke

M'en re-ve-nant de la jo-lie Ro-chel-le,

J'ai re-con-tré trois jo-lies de-moi-sel-les.

C'est l'a-vi-ron qui nous mè-ne, qui nous mè-ne,

C'est l'a-vi-ron qui nous mène en haut.

1. M'en revenant de la jolie Rochelle,
   M'en revenant de la jolie Rochelle,
   J'ai rencontré trois jolies demoiselles.

   REFRAIN:
   C'est l'aviron qui nous mène, qui nous mène,
   C'est l'aviron qui nous mène en haut.

2. J'ai rencontré trois jolies demoiselles;)2
   J'ai point choisi, mais j'ai pris la plus belle.

3. J'ai point choisi, mais j'ai pris la plus belle;)2
   J'y fis monter derrièr' moi, sur ma selle.

4. J'y fis monter derrièr' moi, sur ma selle;)2
   J'y fis cent lieues sans parler avec elle.

5. J'y fis cent lieues sans parler avec elle;)2
   Au bout d'cent lieues, ell' me d'mandit à boire.

6. Au bout d'cent lieues, ell' me d'mandit à boire;)2
   Je l'ai menée auprès d'une fontaine.

7. Je l'ai menée auprès d'une fontaine;)2
   Quand ell' fut là, ell' ne voulut point boire.

8. Quand ell' fut là, ell' ne voulut point boire;)2
   Je l'ai menée au logis de son père.

9. Je l'ai menée au logis de son père;)2
   Quand ell' fut là, ell' buvait à pleins verres.

10. Quand ell' fut là, ell' buvait à pleins verres;)2
    À la santé de son père et sa mère.

11. À la santé de son père et sa mère;)2
    À la santé de ses sœurs et ses frères.

12. À la santé de ses sœurs et ses frères;)2
    À la santé d'celui que son cœur aime.

1. Riding along the road from Rochelle city,
   Riding along the road from Rochelle city,
   I met three girls and all of them were pretty.

CHORUS:
   Pull on the oars as we glide along together,
   Pull on the oars as we glide along.

2. By chance I chose the one who was the beauty,)2
   Lifted her up so she could ride beside me.

3. With ne'er a word we rode along together,)2
   After a while she said, 'I'd like a drink, sir.'

4. Quickly I found a spring from out the mountain,)2
   But she'd not drink the water from the fountain.

5. On we went to find her home and father,)2
   When we got there she drank, but not of water.

6. Many a toast she drank to her dear mother,)2
   Toasted again her sister and her brother.

7. When she had drunk to sister and to brother,)2
   Turning to me, she toasted her own lover.

50. THE 'H'EMMER JANE'

Now 'tis of a young mai-den this sto-ry I tell, And of her young lo-ver, and what them be-fell. Now her lo-ver was a sea cap-tain and he sailed the blue sea, And this is the circumstances surroundin' the de-par-ture of 'e.

1. Now 'tis of a young maiden this story I tell,
   And of her young lover, and what them befell.
   Now her lover was a sea captain and he sailed the blue sea,
   And this is the circumstances surroundin' the departure of 'e.

2. Now the vessel 'e sailed on was called the *H'Emmer Jane*.
   'Twas in riverence of she that he gi'ed her that name,
   So that while 'e was sailin' all o'er the blue sea
   The vessel that 'e sailed in might mind 'e of she.

3. With a boatload of shingles our Captain sailed away,
   Sailed away from his true love all on a summer's day,
   And he never more was heard of, nor his vessel so brave,
   So 'twas figgered pretty ginerally that he found a watery grave.

4. On a cold stormy mornin' all down by the sea
   H'Emmer Jane sot a-waitin', sot a-waitin' for 'e.
   On a cold stormy mornin' her body were found,
   So 'twas figgered pretty ginerally she'd gone crazy and got drowned.

5. They buried her up in the buryin' ground,
   And they put up a headstone tellin' how she were found,
   And over her head they sot out a willer tree
   That the wind in the branches might mind dey of she.

6. Not so very long after these here t'ings occurred
   A stranger comes to town where H'Emmer Jane happened to be bur'd,
   And he axed of the sexton where H'Emmer Jane might be.
   The sexton answered by pointin' to the old willer tree.

7. Next mornin' they found 'im by the side of H'Emmer Jane.
   They found 'is cold carcass insensibly a-layin',
   And in his brist pocket were a handkerchief of her'n,
   So 'twas figgered pretty ginerally 'twas the Captain returned.

8. They buried 'e up in a grave close by 'er,
   And over his head they sot out a wild brier.
   Now the wind in the willer is in memory of she,
   And the wild brier twist round 'en *is in memory of 'e.*

51. THE JOLLY RAFTSMAN O

1. I am sixteen, I do confess,
   I'm sure I am no older O.
   I place my mind, it never shall move,
   It's on a jolly raftsman O.

CHORUS:
   To hew and score it is his plan,
   And handle the broad-axe neatly O.
   It's lay the line and mark the pine
   And do it most completely O.

2. Oh, she is daily scolding me
   To marry some freeholder O.
   I place my mind, it never shall move,
   It's on a jolly raftsman O.

3. My love is marching through the pine
   As brave as Alexander O,
   And none can I find to please my mind
   As well as a jolly raftsman O.

52. THE RED RIVER VALLEY

From this val - ley they say you are go - ing; I shall miss your bright eyes and sweet smile, For a - las you take with you the sun - shine That has bright-ened my path - way a - while.

1. From this valley they say you are going;
   I shall miss your bright eyes and sweet smile,
   For alas you take with you the sunshine
   That has brightened my pathway awhile.

CHORUS:
> *Come and sit by my side if you love me,*
> *Do not hasten to bid me adieu,*
> *But remember the Red River Valley*
> *And the girl who has loved you so true.*

2. For this long, long time I have waited
   For the words that you never would say,
   But now my last hope has vanished
   When they tell me that you're going away.

3. Oh, there never could be such a longing
   In the heart of a white maiden's breast
   As there is in the heart that is breaking
   With love for the boy who came west.

4. When you go to your home by the ocean
   May you never forget the sweet hours
   That we spent in the Red River Valley,
   Or the vows we exchanged 'mid the bowers.

5. Will you think of the valley you're leaving?
   Oh, how lonely and dreary 'twill be!
   Will you think of the fond heart you're breaking
   And be true to your promise to me?

6. The dark maiden's prayer for her lover
   To the spirit that rules o'er the world:
   His pathway with sunshine may cover,
   Leave his grief to the Red River girl.

53. THE YOUNG SPANISH LASS

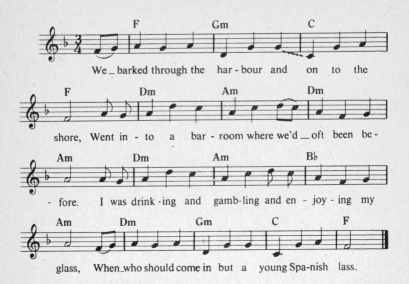

We — barked through the har-bour and on to the shore, Went in-to a bar-room where we'd — oft been be- fore. I was drink-ing and gamb-ling and en - joy - ing my glass, When — who should come in but a young Spa-nish lass.

1. We barked through the harbour and on to the shore,
   Went into a bar-room where we'd oft been before.
   I was drinking and gambling and enjoying my glass,
   When who should come in but a young Spanish lass.

2. She sat down beside me and took up my hand,
   Saying, 'You are a stranger, not one of this land.
   Will you come, jolly sailor, will you roam along with me
   Down in some distant valley beneath a cold northerly?'

3. I quickly decided and with her did go.
   She lived all alone in a sweet little home.
   She was dressed neat and handsome, and her age were sixteen,
   And the name of the Spaniard I think was Irene.

4. It was early next morning our ship she set sail,
   And on to the pier young Irene she came,
   And with her handkerchief she kept wiping her eyes:
   'Don't you dare for to leave me, jolly sailor!' she cries.

5. We barked through the harbour and on to the bay,
   And we bid her farewell as we sailed away.
   'When you reaches Oporto and your own Newfoundland,
   Don't forget of the Spaniard who keeps squeezing your hand.'

54. YOUNG MACDONALD

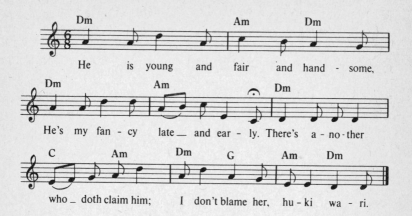

He is young and fair and hand-some, He's my fan-cy late — and ear-ly. There's a-no-ther who — doth claim him; I don't blame her, hu-ki wa-ri.

1. He is young and fair and handsome,
   He's my fancy late and early.
   There's another who doth claim him;
   I don't blame her, huki wari.

CHORUS:

   Aye gratallion, oh gratallion,
   Aye gratallion bounsa guiles,
   Telim meen geneel denoosa
   Thisakerry suas learchin.

2. In the fields he fought the battles,
   Brave enacted western arms.
   There were thousands there to greet him,
   He did spot the malcha goya.

3. You all know this young MacDonald;
   He was brought up here in Glengarry.
   Now he's off to Colorado
   With his name and his metrachee.

VII. TRIALS OF LOVE

55. À LA CLAIRE FONTAINE

English words by Edith Fowke

À la clai-re fon-tai-ne M'en al-lant pro-me-ner, J'ai trou-vé l'eau si bel-le Que je m'y suis bai-gné. *Lui y'a long-temps que je t'ai-me, Ja-mais je ne t'ou-blie-rai.*

1. À la claire fontaine
   M'en allant promener,
   J'ai trouvé l'eau si belle
   Que je m'y suis baigné.

   REFRAIN:
   Lui y'a longtemps que je t'aime,
   Jamais je ne t'oublierai.

2. J'ai trouvé l'eau si belle
   Que je m'y suis baigné;
   Sous les feuilles d'un chêne
   Je me suis fait sécher.

3. Sous les feuilles d'un chêne
   Je me suis fait sécher,
   Sur la plus haute branche
   Le rossignol chantait.

4. Sur la plus haute branche
   Le rossignol chantait.
   Chante, rossignol, chante,
   Toi qui as le cœur gai.

1. By the clear running fountain
   I strayed one summer day.
   The water looked so cooling
   I bathed without delay.

   CHORUS:
   Many long years have I loved you,
   Ever in my heart you'll stay.

2. Beneath an oak tree shady
   I dried myself that day
   When from the topmost branches
   A bird's song came my way.

3. Sing, nightingale, keep singing,
   Your heart is always gay.
   You have no cares to grieve you,
   While I could weep today,

4. You have no cares to grieve you,
   While I could weep today,
   For I have lost my loved one
   In such a senseless way.

5. Chante, rossignol, chante,
   Toi qui as le cœur gai,
   Tu as le cœur à rire,
   Moi, je l'ai t'à pleurer.

6. Tu as le cœur à rire,
   Moi je l'ai t'à pleurer;
   J'ai perdu ma maîtresse
   Sans l'avoir mérité.

7. J'ai perdu ma maîtresse
   Sans l'avoir mérité,
   Pour un bouquet de roses
   Que je lui refusai.

8. Pour un bouquet de roses
   Que je lui refusai.
   Je voudrais que la rose
   Fût encore au rosier.

9. Je voudrais que la rose
   Fût encore au rosier,
   Et mois et ma maîtresse
   Dans les mêm's amitiés.

5. She wanted some red roses
   But I did rudely say
   She could not have the roses
   That I had picked that day.

6. Now I wish those red roses
   Were on their bush today,
   While I and my beloved
   Still went our old sweet way.

56. HARBOUR LE COU

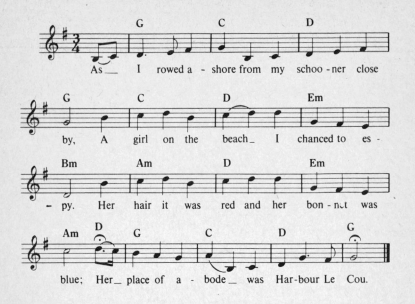

As — I rowed a - shore from my schoo - ner close
by, A girl on the beach — I chanced to es -
- py. Her hair it was red and her bon - net was
blue; Her — place of a - bode — was Har - bour Le Cou.

1. As I rowed ashore from my schooner close by,
   A girl on the beach I chanced to espy.
   Her hair it was red and her bonnet was blue;
   Her place of abode was Harbour Le Cou.

2. O boldly I asked her to walk on the sand.
   She smiled like an angel and held out her hand,
   So I buttoned me guernsey and hove 'way me chew
   In the dark rolling waters of Harbour Le Cou.

3. My ship she lay anchored far out on the tide
   As I strolled along with the maid at my side.
   I told her I loved her; she said, 'I'll be true,'
   As I winked at the moon over Harbour Le Cou.

4. As we walked on the sands at the close of the day
   I thought of my wife who was home in Torbay;
   I knew that she'd kill me if she only knew
   I was courting a lassie in Harbour Le Cou.

5. As we passed a log cabin that stood on the shore
   I met an old comrade I'd sailed with before.
   He treated me kindly, saying, 'Jack, how are you?
   It's seldom I see you in Harbour Le Cou.'

6. And as I was parting, this maiden in tow,
   He broke up my party with one single blow,
   Saying, 'Regards to your missus and wee kiddies two;
   I remember her well, she's from Harbour Le Cou.'

7. I looked at this damsel a-standing 'longside,
   Her jaw it dropped, and her mouth opened wide,
   And then like a she-cat upon me she flew,
   And I fled from the furies of Harbour Le Cou.

8. Come all you young sailors who walk on the shore,
   Beware of old comrades you'd sailed with before.
   Beware of the maiden with bonnet of blue,
   And the pretty young damsels of Harbour Le Cou.

57. THE LONESOME SCENES OF WINTER

As the lone - some scenes of __ win - ter in __ stor - my winds do blow, Clouds a - round the cen - tre in - cline to frost and snow. You're the girl I have cho - sen to be my on - ly . dear; Your scorn - ful heart is __ fro - zen and __ drift - ed far I fear.

1. As the lonesome scenes of winter in stormy winds do blow,
   Clouds around the centre incline to frost and snow.
   You're the girl I have chosen to be my only dear;
   Your scornful heart is frozen and drifted far I fear.

2. One night I went to see my love; she proved most scornfully.
   I asked her if she'd marry; she would not marry me.
   'The night it is far spent, my love, it's near the break of day,
   And I'm waiting for an answer: my dear, what do you say?'

3. 'I can but plainly tell you, I'll lead a single life.
   I never thought it fitting that I should be your wife.
   Now take a civil answer and for yourself provide.
   I have another sweetheart, and you I have laid aside.'

4. Now my mind is changing that old love for the new,
   This wide and lonesome valley I mean to ramble through
   In search of someone handsome that might my fancy fill.
   This world is wide and lonesome; if she don't, another will.

58. THE FALSE YOUNG MAN

'Oh, __ come, sit __ down close to me, my dear, While
I sing you a mer-ry song. ____ 'Tis now for__
us well__ o - ver a year Since to - ge-ther you and
I have_ been;____ Since to - ge-ther you and I have_
been, my dear, Since to - ge-ther you and I __ have_
been.____ 'Tis now for__ us well__ o - ver a
year Since to - ge-ther you and I have__ been.'

1. 'Oh, come, sit down close to me, my
dear,
While I sing you a merry song.
'Tis now for us well over a year
Since together you and I have been;
Since together you and I have been,
my dear,
Since together you and I have been.
'Tis now for us well over a year
Since together you and I have been.'

2. 'I will not sit close to you, my dear,
Now nor at any other time.
You've given your love to another
one,
And your heart no longer is mine.
Your heart no longer is mine, my
dear,
Your heart no longer is mine.
You've given your love to another
one,
And your heart no longer is mine.

3. 'When your heart truly was mine,
      my dear,
   You laid your head upon my breast,
   And I listened to the strange oaths
      you swore
   That the sun it rose in the west;
   That the sun it rose in the west, my
      dear,
   That the sun it rose in the west,
   And I listened to the strange oaths
      you swore
   That the sun it rose in the west.

4. 'There's a rose in the garden for you,
      my dear,
   A rose in the garden for you.
   When fish fly high like the birds in
      the sky
   Young men will then prove true.
   Young men will then prove true, my
      dear,
   Young men will then prove true.
   When fish fly high like the birds in
      the sky,
   Young men will then prove true.'

59. DOWN BY SALLY'S GARDEN

You— ramb - ling boys of plea - sure, give ear to those few lines I write, Al - though I'm a ro - ver, and in rov - ing I take great de - light. I set my mind on a hand - some girl who oft - times did — me slight, But my mind was ne - ver ea - sy till my dar - ling were in my sight.

1. You rambling boys of pleasure, give ear to those few lines I write,
   Although I'm a rover, and in roving I take great delight.
   I set my mind on a handsome girl who ofttimes did me slight,
   But my mind was never easy till my darling were in my sight.

2. It was down by Sally's garden one evening late I took my way.
   'Twas there I spied this pretty little girl, and those words to me sure she did say;
   She advised me to take love easy, as the leaves grew on the tree,
   But I was young and foolish, with my darling could not agree.

3. The very next time I met my love, sure I thought her heart was mine,
   But as the weather changes, my true love she changed her mind.
   Cursed gold is the root of evil, oh it shines with a glittering hue,
   Causes many the lad and lass to part, let their hearts be ever so true.

4. Sure I wish I was in Dublin town, and my true love along with me,
   With money to support us and keep us in good company,
   With lots of liquor plentiful, flowing bowls on every side.
   Let fortune never daunt you, my love, we're both young and the world is wide.

5. But there's one thing more that grieves me sore is to be called a runaway,
   And to leave the spot I was born in, oh Cupid cannot set me free,
   And to leave that darling girl I love, oh, alas, what will I do?
   Will I become a rover, sleep with the girl I never knew?

60. AN OLD MAN HE COURTED ME

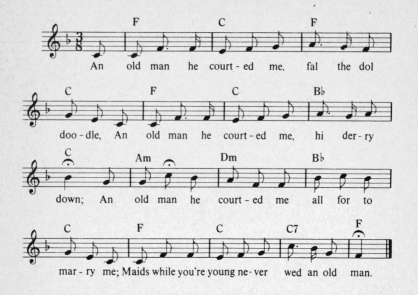

An old man he court-ed me, fal the dol
doo-dle, An old man he court-ed me, hi der-ry
down; An old man he court-ed me all for to
mar-ry me; Maids while you're young ne-ver wed an old man.

1. An old man he courted me, fal the dol doodle,
   An old man he courted me, hi derry down;
   An old man he courted me all for to marry me;
   Maids while you're young never wed an old man.

2. For he has no fal the dol all the dol doodle,
   Oh, he has no fal the dol diddle the one.
   He has no filoodle, he's lost his ding-doodle,
   So maids while you're young never wed an old man.

3. It's when that we went to church, fal the dol doodle,
   It's when that we went to church, hi derry down,
   It's when that we went to church he left me in the lurch;
   Maids while you're young never wed an old man.

4. It's when we were coming home, fal the dol doodle,
   Oh, when we were coming home, hi derry down,
   It's when we were coming home he let me walk alone;
   Maids while you're young never wed an old man.

5. It's when at supper set, fal the dol doodle,
   When at supper set, hi derry down,
   It's when at supper set devil a bite he could eat;
   Maids while you're young never wed an old man.

6. Oh, it's when that we went to bed, fal the dol doodle,
   Oh, when that we went to bed, hi derry down,
   It's when that we went to bed, he lay as if he was dead;
   Maids while you're young never wed an old man.

7. I threw me leg over him, fal the dol doodle,
   I threw me leg over him, hi derry down,
   I threw me leg over him, I swore I would smother him;
   Maids while you're young never wed an old man.

8. Oh, it's when he fell fast asleep, fal the dol doodle,
   Oh, when he fell fast asleep, hi derry down,
   It's when he fell fast asleep, out of bed I did creep,
   And into the arms of a sporting young man.

9. Oh, there we did sport and play, fal the dol doodle,
   Oh, there we did sport and play, hi derry down,
   It's there we did sport and play until the break of day;
   Then I crept back to my lazy old man.

61. THE WEAVER

Oh, as I roved out one moon-light night, The stars were shin — ing and all things bright. I spied a pret-ty maid by the light of the moon, And un-der her ap - ron she car-ried a loom. *To me right whack fal the doo - a di - do - day, Right whack fal the doo - a di - do - day, Too - ra loo - ra loo - ra lay, To me right whack fal the doo - a di - do - day.*

1. Oh, as I roved out one moonlight night,
   The stars were shining and all things bright.
   I spied a pretty maid by the light of the moon,
   And under her apron she carried a loom.

CHORUS:
   To me right whack fal the doo-a di-do-day,
   Right whack fal the doo-a di-do-day,
   Too-ra loo-ra loo-ra lay,
   To me right whack fal the doo-a di-do-day.

2. She says, 'Young man, what trade do you bear?'
   Says I, 'I'm a weaver, I do declare.
   I am a weaver, brisk and free.'
   'Would you weave upon my loom, kind sir?' said she.

3. There was Nancy Right and Nancy Rill:
   For them I wove the Diamond Twill;
   Nancy Blue and Nancy Brown:
   For them I wove the Rose and the Crown.

4. So I laid her down upon the grass,
   I braced her loom both tight and fast,
   And for to finish it with a joke,
   I topped it off with double stroke.

62. NELLIE COMING HOME FROM THE WAKE

Oh, pret - ty lit - tle Nel - - lie, the milk - maid so gay, Be - ing fond of going to a ball____ or a spree. Says the mis - sus un - to Nel - lie, 'I would have you to be - ware. When you go to the spree, Joe Ro - gers he'll be there. He will take you in his arms and he'll keep you from all harm, And per - haps you might be sor - ry go - ing home___ in the morn.' *Mush - a - na, fal the day.*

(Note: Verses 2 to 5 omit bars between ★ and ★★.)

1. Oh, pretty little Nellie, the milkmaid so gay,
   Being fond of going to a ball or a spree.
   Says the missus unto Nellie, 'I would have you to beware.
   When you go to the spree, Joe Rogers he'll be there.
   He will take you in his arms and he'll keep you from all harm,
   And perhaps you might be sorry going home in the morn.'

CHORUS:
Mush-a-na, fal the day.

2. Nellie she got ready and away she did steer,
   Praying all the time that Joe Rogers would be there,
   That he would take her in his arms and keep her from all harm.
   Then she knew she wouldn't be sorry going home in the morn.

3. When she got there, she got brandy, rum and cake –
   She never got such usage before or at a wake.
   Rogers took her in his arms and he kept her from all harm,
   Saying, 'I know you won't be sorry going home in the morn.'

4. Early in the morning, just at the break of day,
   He laid Nellie down beside the stack of hay.
   Says Rogers unto Nellie, 'I laid you down so neat,
   Sure I'll play you "Shoot the Cat" coming home from the wake.'

5. Eight months was over and nine coming on,
   Nellie she gave birth to a darling young son.
   Says the missus unto Nellie, 'I will christen him for your sake,
   And we'll call it "Shoot the Cat" coming home from the wake.'

63. SHE'S LIKE THE SWALLOW

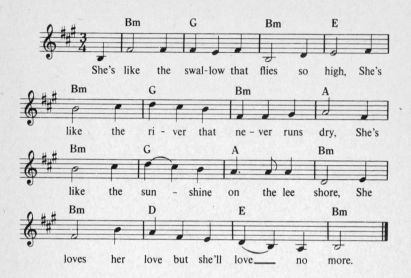

She's like the swal-low that flies so high, She's like the ri - ver that ne - ver runs dry, She's like the sun - shine on the lee shore, She loves her love but she'll love no more.

1. She's like the swallow that flies so high,
   She's like the river that never runs dry,
   She's like the sunshine on the lee shore,
   She loves her love but she'll love no more.

2. 'Twas down in the meadow this fair maid bent
   A-picking the primrose just as she went.
   The more she picked and the more she pulled,
   Until she gathered her apron full.

3. She climbed on yonder hill above
   To give a rose unto her love.
   She gave him one, she gave him three,
   She gave her heart for company.

4. And as they sat on yonder hill
   His heart grew hard, so harder still.
   He has two hearts instead of one.
   She says, 'Young man, what have you done?'

5. 'How foolish, foolish you must be
   To think I love no one but thee.
   The world's not made for one alone,
   I take delight in everyone.'

6. She took her roses and made a bed,
   A stony pillow for her head.
   She lay her down, no more did say,
   But let her roses fade away.

7. She's like the swallow that flies so high,
   She's like the river that never runs dry,
   She's like the sunshine on the lee shore,
   She loves her love but she'll love no more.

VIII. BRITISH BROADSIDES

64. THE BONNY BUNCH OF RUSHES GREEN

As I roved out one May mor-ning,— to the green— fields I took— my way, With my two bea-gles roar— ing, ex - pect-ing there some game to see. It was there I spied— my Ma - ry, she was fair - er than an A-ra - bi - an queen; She was at her dai - ly la - bour,— a- - reap - ing of her— ru – shes green.

1. As I roved out one May morning, to the green fields I took my way,
   With my two beagles roaring, expecting there some game to see.
   It was there I spied my Mary, she was fairer than an Arabian queen;
   She was at her daily labour, a-reaping of her rushes green.

2. I stood and looked all round me, no other one there could I see
   But me and my love Mary; I embraced her most tenderly.
   She says, 'Young man, be easy, don't tease me but let me be;
   Don't you toss my rushes carelessly, great labour they have been to me.'

3. 'If I toss your rushes carelessly, it's more than I intend to do.
   If I toss your rushes carelessly, a bonny bunch I'll reap for you.'
   'Come sit you down beside me, although you have led me astray;
   Come sit you down beside me for the dew has scarce all gone away.'

4. So me and my love Mary sat down under a laurel tree
   Where the small birds joined in chorus; their notes were in high Germany.
   The thrush he joined in chorus while I embraced my Arabian queen;
   It's you I mean, my Mary, and your bonny bunch of rushes green.

5. They kissed, shook hands, and parted, although they were to meet again
   To join their hands in wedlock bands and never more to part again.
   It's now they have got married, they're out of sorrow, grief, and pain,
   And he enjoys his Mary and her bonny bunch of rushes green.

65. THE SAILOR'S RETURN

A la - dy walked in yon -der gar – den,
A gen - tle -man chan – céd to pass by.
He stepped up to her for to view her; Says he, 'Fair maid, do you fan - cy I?'

1. A lady walked in yonder garden,
   A gentleman chancéd to pass by.
   He stepped up to her for to view her;
   Says he, 'Fair maid, do you fancy I?'

2. 'Oh, I fancy you as a man of honour,
   A man of honour you seem to be.
   You might have married some rich young lady,
   And had your servants to wait on ye.'

3. 'Oh, do you see on to yonder castle,
   The sun does shine on every side?
   I'll make you mistress of all that's yonder
   If you consent for to be my bride.'

4. 'Oh, what cares I for your gold or silver,
   Or what cares I for your house or land,
   Or what cares I for this world's pleasure,
   If my poor sailor would return?'

5. 'Oh, do you say that you love a sailor,
   Or do you say that you love a slave?
   Perhaps your sailor lies dead and rolling
   In some watery ocean for to be his grave.'

6. 'Oh, if he's alive, I do dearly love him,
   And if he's dead, I wish him rest.
   Oh, for his sake I'll never marry,
   For he's the one that I love best.'

7. He put his hand all into his pocket,
   His fingers being both long and small;
   He pulled out a ring that was broke between them;
   When she saw this, down she did fall.

8. 'Rise up, rise up, my own true lover,
   And take these jewels from my hand,
   For I've brought home both gold and silver,
   The briny ocean no more to cross.'

9. 'Are you my true and single lover?
   Your ways and features do not agree,
   But seven long years make an alteration;
   It's been seven long years since you sailed from me.'

10. Oh, now she's got her own true lover,
    Her own true dear from off her heart.
    Happy may they both live together
    Till death does cause them for to part.

66. THE PLAINS OF WATERLOO

As__ I roved__ out on__ a fine sum-mer's
mor-ning Down by__ the gay banks of a clear pur-ling
stream, I es-pied a love-ly maid mak-ing
sad la-men-ta-tion; I threw my-self in
am-bush to hear__ her sad strain. Through the
grove she marched a-long, caused the val-leys to
ring__ O, The small feathered song-sters all round her they
flew, Saying, 'The war is all o-ver and peace it is re-
-stored a-gain, But my Wil-lie is not re-
-turn-ing from the plains of Wa-ter-loo.'

1. As I roved out on a fine summer's morning
   Down by the gay banks of a clear purling stream,
   I espied a lovely maid making sad lamentation;
   I threw myself in ambush to hear her sad strain.
   Through the grove she marched along, caused the valleys to ring O,
   The small feathered songsters all round her they flew,
   Saying, 'The war is all over and peace it is restored again,
   But my Willie is not returning from the plains of Waterloo.'

2. I stepped up to this fair one and says, 'My fond creature,
   Dare I make so bold as to ask your lover's name?
   For I have been in battle where cannons around do rattle,
   And by your descriptions I might have known the same.'
   'Willie Smith's my true love's name; he's a hero of great fame.
   He has gone and he's left me in sorrow, it's true.
   No one shall me enjoy but my own darling boy,
   And yet he's not returning from the plains of Waterloo.'

3. 'If Willie Smith's your true love's name, he's a hero of great fame.
   He and I have been in battle through many's the long campaign:
   Through Italy and Russia, through Germany and Prussia,
   He was my loyal comrade through France and through Spain.
   Until at length by the French, oh that we were surrounded;
   Like the heroes of old we did them subdue.
   We fought for three days till at length we did defeat him,
   That brave Napoleon Boney on the plains of Waterloo.

4. 'Oh, the eighteenth day of June, it ended the battle
   And left many a fine hero to sigh and to moan.
   The war drums did beat and the cannons aloud did rattle;
   'Twas by a French soldier your Willie he was slain,
   And as I passed by, oh, where he lay a-bleeding,
   I scarcely had time to bid him adieu.
   With a faltering voice, oh, these words he was repeating:
   "Farewell, my lovely Annie, you are far from Waterloo".'

5. Oh, when this lovely maid heard this sad acclamation,
   Her two rosy cheeks they grew pale into one.
   When I saw this handsome maid in such sad lamentation,
   I says, 'My lovely Annie, I am the very one,
   And here is the ring which between us was broken,
   In the midst of all dangers to remind me of you,'
   And when she saw the token she flew into my arms,
   Saying, 'You're welcome, dearest Willie, from the plains of *Waterloo*.'

67. WILL O'RILEY

Oh,— as I roved out —one e-ve-ning down by yon ri-ver - side, I es - pied a— hand - some girl, and the tears rolled from her eyes. 'This is a cold and— storm-y night,' these words I heard her say, 'And my— love is on— the rag-ing sea; he is bound for A - me - ri - cay.

1. Oh, as I roved out one evening down by yon riverside,
   I espied a handsome girl, and the tears rolled from her eyes.
   'This is a cold and stormy night,' these words I heard her say,
   'And my love is on the raging sea; he is bound for Americay.

2. 'Will O'Riley was my true love's name; his age was scarce nineteen.
   He was as nice a young man as ever my eyes have seen.
   My father he's got riches great, but Riley he is poor,
   And because I love my sailor boy they cannot me endure.

3. 'Oh my mamma took me by the hand, these words to me did say:
   "If you be fond of O'Riley, 'tis send him far away.
   Oh, if you love young Riley, have him leave this counterie,
   For your father swears he will have his life or you'll shun his company."

4. 'Oh, 'tis mother dear, don't be severe, where can I send my love?
   My very heart lies in his breast, as constant as a dove.'
   "O daughter dear, I'm not severe; here is five hundred pound.
   Send O'Riley to Americay and he'll purchase there some ground." '

5. Oh, when Ella got the money, straight to O'Riley she did run,
   Saying, 'Riley, lovelie Riley, here is five hundred pounds.
   Five hundred pounds in gold,' said she, 'my mamma sent to you.
   You sail away to Americay and I will follow you.'

6. It was early the next morning he was to sail away,
   But before he put a foot on board these words to her did say:
   'Here is a token of true love; I'll now break it in two.
   You have half my heart and half this ring until I will make out you.'

7. Now the ship at last in the harbour all for to sail away;
   Stormy were those waters and the waves rolled mountains high.
   The ship was wrecked, all on board was lost, which grieved her parients sore.
   Will O'Riley in his true love's arms lay drowned upon the shore.

8. There was a letter in her bosom and it was wrote with blood,
   Saying, 'Cruel were my parients, they sent away my love.'
   Come all of you fair maidens and a warning take by me:
   'Tis never let the boy you love sail to Amer*icay*.

68. THE GREEN BRIER SHORE

Oh,—then I can court lit-tle and I can court long,
And I'll court an old sweet-heart—— till the
new one comes a-long. I'll kiss them and
court them—— keep their mind at ease, But when
their back is turn-ing I'll court who I please.

1. Oh, then I can court little and I can court long,
   And I'll court an old sweetheart till the new one comes along.
   I'll kiss them and court them – keep their mind at ease,
   But when their back is turning I'll court who I please.

2. At the foot of yon mountain where the fountain do flow,
   Where the primrose and daisies in splendour do grow,
   'Twas there I spied a fair maid, she's the one I adore,
   And to be parted from her 'twould grieve my heart sore.

3. 'Oh, it's Nancy, lovely Nancy, you're the girl I adore,
   And to be parted from you, 'twould grieve my heart sore.
   Your parients are rich, love, and angry with me,
   But if they should part us, it's ruined I'd be.'

4. 'Oh, it's Willie, lovely Willie, you're the boy I adore,
   And to be parted from you, 'twould grieve my heart sore.
   Your looks they do please me, and I'll ask nothing more,
   But I will go with you to the green brier shore.'

158

5. 'Oh, Nancy, lovely Nancy, your parients are rich,
   And I've got no fortune, that troubles me much.
   Your friends and relations, they would mourn for your sake
   If you were to leave them and follow a rake.'

6. 'There's a tree in my father's garden, lovely (Willie),' says she,
   'Where the ladies and gentlemen do wait on me,
   And when they are all sleeping and silent at rest,
   You can come to my arms; you're the boy I love *best*.'

69. THE BONNY LABOURING BOY

Oh, John - ny was my true love's name as
you can plain - ly see, And my fa - ther he em -
ployed him his la - bouring boy to be, To
har - row, reap, and to sow the seed, and to
plough my fa - ther's land; Ve - ry soon I fell in
love with him as you may un - der - stand.

1. Oh, Johnny was my true love's name as you can plainly see,
   And my father he employed him his labouring boy to be,
   To harrow, reap, and to sow the seed, and to plough my father's land;
   Very soon I fell in love with him as you may understand.

2. I courted him for six long months but little did I know
   That cruel was my father; he proved my overthrow.
   He watched us close one evening down by a shady grove
   While pledging our vows together in the constant bands of love.

3. My mother come to me one day and this to me did say:
   'Oh, your father is determined for to appoint your wedding day.'
   Well nobly I made answer, 'It's with him I'll never comply,
   For I'd rather live a single life or have my labouring boy.'

4. 'O daughter, dearest daughter, oh why do you talk so strange,
   To marry a poor labouring boy the wide world for to range?
   Some noble lord would fancy you better; great riches you could enjoy,
   So do not throw your life away for a poor labouring boy.'

5. 'O mother, dearest mother, your talk is all in vain.
   Your kings, lords, dukes or earls, their offer I'd disdain.
   I'd rather live a single life, my time for to enjoy,
   Then increasing nature prosper for my bonny labouring boy.'

6. Five hundred pounds of my best clothes I sold that very night,
   And with the boy who I love best to Belfast we did fly.
   His love it has entangled me and the same I'll never deny,
   And God may speed the plough with my bonny labouring boy.

7. So fill your glasses to the brim, let the toast go merrily round;
   Here is a health to every labouring man who ploughs and sows the ground,
   And when his work is over, it's home he'll speed with joy,
   And happy, happy is the girl who weds the labouring boy.

70. THE SHIP'S CARPENTER

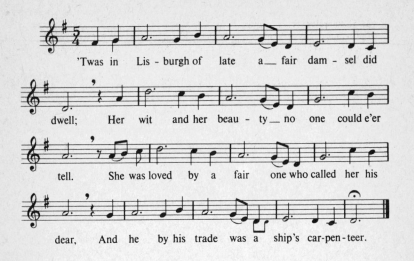

'Twas in Lis-burgh of late a — fair dam - sel did dwell; Her wit and her beau - ty — no one could e'er tell. She was loved by a fair one who called her his dear, And he by his trade was a ship's car-pen-teer.

1. 'Twas in Lisburgh of late a fair damsel did dwell;
   Her wit and her beauty no one could e'er tell.
   She was loved by a fair one who called her his dear,
   And he by his trade was a ship's carpenteer.

2. He says, 'Molly, lovely Molly, if you will agree
   And give your consent, love, for to marry me,
   Your love it would cure me from all sorrow and care
   If you will agree to wed a ship's carpenter.'

3. 'Twas changing and blushing like a rose in full bloom,
   'To marry you, Willie, you know I'm too young.
   I'm afraid for to venture before I prepare;
   I never will marry a ship's carpenter.'

4. Her talk was in vain as he straight took denial,
   And he by his coming soon made her reply.
   'Twas by her exception he led her astray;
   O'er high hills and pathways he did her betray.

5. Things passed on for awhile till at length we did hear
   A ship must be sailing all o'er the salt sea.
   It grieved this fair damsel and wounded her heart
   To think from her darling how soon must she part.

6. She says, 'Willie, lovely Willie, are you going on sea?
   Remember those vows that you once made to me.
   If at home you don't tarry I can find no rest.
   Oh, how can you leave your poor darling at last?'

7. With tender expression those words he did say:
   'I will marry you, Molly, before I go away.
   If it be tomorrow, and you will come down,
   A ring I will buy you worth one hundred pound.'

8. With tender expression they parted that night;
   They promised to meet the next morning by light.
   Says Willie to Molly, 'You must come with me
   And before we are married my friends for to see.'

9. He led her through pathways o'er hills that were steep
   Till this pretty fair one began for to weep,
   Saying, 'False-hearted Willie, you've led me astray,
   Purpose my innocent life to betray.'

10. He says, 'You have guessed right; on earth can't you see
    For all of last night I've been digging your grave.'
    When innocent Molly she heard him say so,
    Tears from her eyes like a fountain did flow.

11. 'Twas a grave with a spade lying there she did spy
    Which caused her to sigh and to weep bitterly.
    'O false-hearted Willie, you're the worst of mankind.
    Is this the bride's bed I expected to find?

12. ' 'Tis pity my infant and spare me my life;
    Let me live full of shame if I can't be your wife.
    Take not my life, for my soul you'll betray
    And you (to perdition) soon hurried away.'

13. There's no time to be waiting, disputing to stand.
    He instantly taking a knife in his hand,
    He pierced her bosom and the blood down did flow,
    And into the grave her poor body he throwed.

14. He covered her over and then hurried home,
    Leaving none but the small birds her fate to be known.
    He then sailed on board without more delay;
    He sad sailed for Plowmount far o'er the salt sea.

15. 'Twas a young man named Stewart with courage so brave,
    The night it was dark as he went to the grave.
    A beauty fair damsel to him did appear,
    She held in her arrums an infant most dear.

16. Being merry with liquor, he ran to embrace,
    Transported with joy at her beautiful face,
    But by his amazement she vanished away.
    He told to the captain without more delay.

17. The captain soon summoned his jolly ship's crew.
    'Oh my brave young fellows, I fear some of you
    Has murdered that fair one and then come with me;
    Her poor spirit haunts you all o'er the salt sea.'

18. Then false-hearted Willie he fell to his knees
    And the blood in his veins all like horror did freeze,
    Crying, 'Monster, oh lover, oh what have I done?
    God help me, I fear my poor soul is undone.

19. 'You poor injured fair one, your pardon I crave;
    How soon must I follow you down to the grave!
    There's none but you, fair one, to see that sad sight.'
    And by her distraction *he died the same night*.

71. JAMIE FOYER

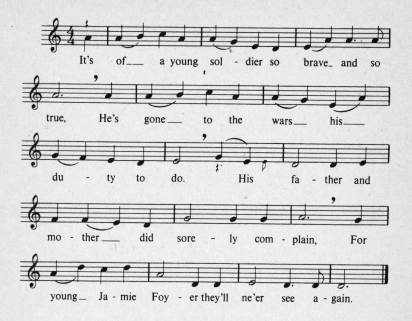

It's of__ a young sol - dier so brave_ and so true, He's gone __ to the wars__ his__ du - ty to do. His fa - ther and mo - ther __ did sore - ly com - plain, For young__ Ja - mie Foy - er they'll ne'er see a - gain.

1. It's of a young soldier so brave and so true,
   He's gone to the wars his duty to do.
   His father and mother did sorely complain,
   For young Jamie Foyer they'll ne'er see again.

2. It's mounting a ladder to scale the wall,
   A shot from a French gun caused Foyer to fall.
   He fell from the ladder like a soldier so brave,
   And young Jamie Foyer in battle was slain.

3. 'If ever you return to Scotland again,
   Tell my dear father I'll never return,
   And alas my poor mother, that long may she mourn,
   For her young son Foyer will never return.'

4. They had for his winding sheet his tartan and plaid,
   And in the cold ground his body they laid.
   With their hearts full of sorrow they covered his grave,
   And young Foyer's comrades marched slowly away.

72. THE BANKS OF THE NILE

'O hark, my love, the drums do beat and
I must haste a - way. The bu - gles sweet - ly
sound - ing, I can no long - er stay, For
I am bound for Ports - mouth, it's
ma - ny a long, long mile,— For to join the Bri - tish
ar - my on the banks— of the Nile.'

1. 'O hark, my love, the drums do beat and I must haste away.
   The bugles sweetly sounding, I can no longer stay,
   For I am bound for Portsmouth, it's many a long, long mile,
   For to join the British army on the banks of the Nile.'

2. 'I'll dress myself in velveteen, I'll go along with you;
   I'll volunteer as servant, I'll go to England, too.
   I'll fight beneath your banners, in fortune on you smile;
   I'll be your loving comrade on the banks of the Nile.'

3. 'Your fingers are too slender, love, your waist it is too small;
   Your precious form it is too weak to stand a cannon ball.
   Your precious form it is too weak to stand such a hard climate,
   Or the sultry suns of Africa yòur precious blood to spoil.'

4. Oh, cursed, cursed be the day that ever war began;
   It's taken away from Canada full many a gallant man.
   It's taken away our Home Guard, protectors of our soil,
   And their bodies feed the worms now on the banks of the Nile.

73. NINE YEARS A SOLDIER

Nine years a - go since I was dig - ging land With two
brogues on my feet and a sho - vel in my hand. Says
I to my - self, 'What a pit - y for to see Such a
neat I - rish lad - die dig - ging turf all the dee.'
Mush - a doo doo - i - a, sing - ing fal the doo - i - ad - dy, Mush - a
doo doo - i - a, sing - ing fal the doo - i - ay.

★(Note: Verses 3 and 7 go straight to Chorus from here.)

1. Nine years ago since I was digging land
   With two brogues on my feet and a shovel in my hand.
   Says I to myself, 'What a pity for to see
   Such a neat Irish laddie digging turf all the dee.'

CHORUS:
Mush a doo doo-i-a, singing fal the doo-i-addy
Mush a doo doo-i-a, singing fal the doo-i-ay.

2. I brushed up my brogues and shook hands with my spade
   And I off to the fair like a courting young blade.
   The first man I met he asked me to 'list;
   Says I, 'Gramachree, give a soldier your fist.'

3. The next man I met he gave me a long coat
   With a stiff stock of leather right under my throat.

4. The next man I met he gave me a long gun,
   Under the trigger I placed my left thumb.
   First come fire and then come smoke,
   For it gave my shoulder such a devil of a poke.

5. The next thing he gave me was a sorrel horse,
   All bridled, all saddled, I threw my legs across.
   Into his sides I stuck my steel,
   For the stiff-legged devil he would run through the field.

6. On Vinegar Hill I had very bad luck:
   My brogues full of sand stuck into the muck.
   I stood on my head for fear of being shot,
   And I fell on my belly and went flop, flop, flop.

7. Nine years a soldier, thank God it wasn't ten!
   I'll go back to old Ireland and dig murphies again.

74. THE ENNISKILLEN DRAGOON

1. A beautiful damsel of fame and renown,
   A gentleman's daughter of fame and renown –
   As she rode by the barracks, this beautiful maid,
   She stood in her coach to see the dragoons on parade.

2. They were all dressed out like gentlemen's sons,
   With their bright shining swords and their carabine guns,
   With their silver-mounted pistols she observed them full soon
   Because that she loved her Enniskillen dragoon.

3. You bright sons of Mars who stand on the right,
   Whose armour does shine like the bright stars of night,
   Saying, 'Willie, dearest Willie, you've 'listed full soon
   For to serve as a Royal Enniskillen Dragoon.'

4. 'O Flora, dearest Flora, your pardon do I crave.
   It's now and forever I must be a slave.
   Your parents they insulted me both morning, night and noon
   For fear that you would wed an Enniskillen dragoon.'

5. 'O Willie, dearest Willie, oh mind what you say,
   For children are bound, you know, their parents to obey,
   For when we're leaving Ireland they will change their tune,
   Saying, "The Lord be with you, Enniskillen dragoon".'

6. Fare you well, Enniskillen, fare you well for a while,
   And all round the borders of Erin's green isle,
   And when the war is over, we'll return in full bloom,
   And they'll all welcome home the Enniskillen dragoon.

IX. ANCIENT BALLADS

75. THE FARMER AND THE DEVIL

There was a wee far-mer who lived in this town

(whistle — — — —) There

was a wee far-mer who lived in this town, And he

tore up the ground, the de-vil knows how.

Right toor-i roor-i rip-or-ad-dy down day.

1. There was a wee farmer who lived in this town (*whistle*),
   There was a wee farmer who lived in this town,
   And he tore up the ground, the devil knows how.

CHORUS:
   Right toor-i-roor-i rip-or-addy down day.

2. The Devil came up to him one day (*whistle*),
   The Devil came up to him one day,
   Saying, 'One of your family must come my way.'

3. 'Oh, surely it's not my eldest son (*whistle*),
   Oh, surely it's not my eldest son,
   For if it is I am undone.'

4. 'Oh, no, it's not your oldest son (*whistle*),
   Oh, no, it's not your oldest son.
   It's your scolding wife, and she must come.'

5. He hoist the old woman upon his back (*whistle*),
   He hoist the old woman upon his back,
   And like a bold pedlar he carried his pack.

6. Oh, in he came to hell's back door (*whistle*),
   Oh, in he came to hell's back door;
   He threw her in upon the floor.

7. Up stepped a little devil a-rattling a chain (*whistle*),
   Up stepped a little devil a-rattling a chain;
   She up with her leg and knocked out his brain.

8. Up stepped a little devil behind the wall (*whistle*),
   Up stepped a little devil behind the wall,
   Saying, 'Take her away or she'll kill us all.'

9. Oh, women they are worse than men (*whistle*),
   Oh, women they are worse than men:
   They'll go down to hell and come back again!

76. SEVEN GYPSIES ON YON HILL

Se - ven gyp - sies on yon hill, They were nei - ther bright nor bon - ny O, But they sang so sweet with the chang-ing of their notes That they stole Lord Cas - tle's __ la - dy O.

1. Seven gypsies on yon hill,
   They were neither bright nor bonny O,
   But they sang so sweet with the changing of their notes
   That they stole Lord Castle's lady O.

2. When Lord Castle he came home
   He inquired for his lady O,
   But the waiting-maid she thus replied:
   'She is gone with a gypsy laddie O.'

3. 'Come saddle to me my milk-white steed,
   The bay is not so speedy O,
   And I'll ride east and I'll ride west
   Till I overtake my lady O.'

4. So he rode east and he rode west
   Till he came near Niceree valley O,
   And there he met a poor old man;
   He was both weary and tired O.

5. 'Have you been east and have you been west?
   Have you been to Niceree valley O?
   And did you see my lady fair,
   And is she going with a gypsy laddie O?'

6. 'Yes, I've been east and I've been west,
   And I've been to Niceree valley O,
   And there I saw your lady fair,
   And she was staying with a gypsy laddie O.'

7. So he rode east and he rode west
   Till he came to Niceree valley O,
   And there he found his lady fair,
   And she was going with a gypsy laddie O.

8. 'Will you come home, my dear?' he said,
   'Will you come home, my honey O?
   And by the point of my broadsword
   Not a gypsy shall ever come nigh thee O.'

9. 'No, I won't go home, my dear,' she said,
   'Nor I won't go home, my honey O,
   For I'd rather have a kiss from a gypsy laddie's lips
   Than all Lord Castle's body O.'

10. 'Will you forsake your house and land?
    Will you forsake your baby, too?
    Will you forsake your own dear lord
    And go with a gypsy laddie O?'

11. 'Yes, I'll forsake my house and land,
    And I'll forsake my baby, too,
    And I'll forsake my own dear lord
    And go with a gypsy laddie O.

12. 'Last night I slept on a bed of down,
    Me and my honey O,
    But tonight I'll sleep on a cold barn floor
    With nothing but gypsies around me O.

13. 'They gave to me the honey sweet,
    And they gave to me the sugar, too,
    But I gave to them far better things:
    I gave seven gold rings from my fingers O.'

14. Seven gypsies on yon hill,
    They were neither bright nor bonny O
    But they all came down for to die
    For the stealing of Lord Castle's lady O.

77. THE DEWY DELLS OF YARROW

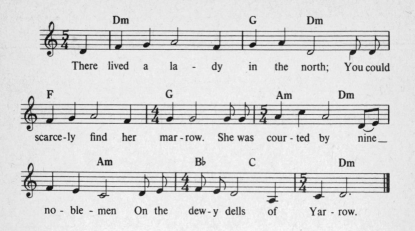

There lived a la-dy in the north; You could
scarce-ly find her mar-row. She was cour-ted by nine_
no-ble-men On the dew-y dells of Yar-row.

1. There lived a lady in the north;
   You could scarcely find her marrow.
   She was courted by nine noblemen
   On the dewy dells of Yarrow.

2. Her father had a bonny ploughboy
   And she did love him dearly.
   She dressed him up like a noble lord
   For to fight for her on Yarrow.

3. She kissed his cheek, she kamed his hair,
   As oft she had done before O.
   She gilted him with a right good sword
   For to fight for her on Yarrow.

4. As he climbed up yon high hill
   And they came down the other,
   There he spied nine noblemen
   On the dewy dells of Yarrow.

5. 'Did you come here for to drink red wine,
   Or did you come here to borrow?
   Or did you come here with a single sword
   For to fight for her on Yarrow?'

6. 'I came not here for to drink red wine,
   And I came not here to borrow,
   But I came here with a single sword
   For to fight for her on Yarrow.

7. 'There are nine of you and one of me,
   And that's but an even number,
   But it's man to man I'll fight you all
   And die for her on Yarrow.'

8. Three he drew and three he slew
   And two lie deadly wounded,
   When a stubborn knight crept up behind
   And pierced him with his arrow.

9. 'Go home, go home, my false young man,
   And tell your sister Sarah
   That her true lover John lies dead and gone
   On the dewy dells of Yarrow.'

10. As he gaed down yon high hill
    And she came down the other,
    It's then he met his sister dear
    A-coming fast to Yarrow.

11. 'O brother dear, I had a dream last night,' she said.
    'I can read it into sorrow:
    Your true lover John lies dead and gone
    On the dewy dells of Yarrow.'

12. This maiden's hair was three-quarters long,
    The colour of it was yellow.
    She tied it around his middle side
    And carried him home to Yarrow.

13. She kissed his cheeks, she kamed his hair
    As oft she had done before O.
    Her true lover John lies dead and gone
    And she carried him home from Yarrow.

14. 'O father dear, you have seven sons;
    You can wed them all tomorrow,
    For the fairest flower amongst them all
    Is the one that died on Yarrow.

15. 'O mother dear, make me my bed,
    And make it long and narrow,
    For the one that died for me today,
    I shall die for him tomorrow.'

78. WILLIE DROWNED IN ERO

1. My Willie is brave, my Willie is tall,
   My Willie is one that is bonny.
   > He promised that he'd marry me
   > If ever he'd marry any,
   > If ever he'd marry any,
   > He promised that he'd marry me
   > If ever he'd marry any.

2. My Willie is to them huntings gone,
   I fear he's gone to tarry.
   > He sent a letter back to me
   > Saying he was too young to marry,
   > Saying he was too young to marry,
   > He sent a letter back to me
   > Saying he was too young to marry.

3. Last night I dreamed a dreadful dream,
   I fear it will bring sorrow.
        I dreamed I was reaping the heather so green
        Down by the banks of Ero . . .

4. 'Well, I will read your dream to you,
   I'll read it with grief and sorrow,
        That before tomorrow night you hear
        Of your Willie being drowned in Ero.' . . .

5. I sought him east, I sought him west,
   I sought him through a valley,
        And underneath the edge of a rock
        Was the corpse of my Willie lying . . .

6. Her hair was full three-quarters long,
   The colour it was yellow,
        And around the waist of her Willie she turned
        To pull him out of Ero . . .

7. They buried him the very next day,
   They buried him with grief and sorrow.
        They buried him the very next day
        Upon the banks of Ero . . .

79. JENNY GO GENTLE

Wil-lie mar-ried a wife and he brought her home,
Jen-ny go gen-tle, Rose Mol-ly. He
might as well have left her a-lone, As the
dew flies o - ver the green val - ley.

1. Willie married a wife and he brought her home,
   Jenny go gentle, Rose Molly.
   He might as well have left her alone,
   As the dew flies over the green valley.

2. Willie went out to follow the plough,
   Jenny go gentle, Rose Molly.
   At noon he came in: 'Is dinner ready now?'
   As the dew flies over the green valley.

3. 'Oh, what says that ugly old elf?'
   Jenny go gentle, Rose Molly.
   'If you want any dinner, you can get it yourself.'
   As the dew flies over the green valley.

4. Then Willie took a knife and went to the fold,
   Jenny go gentle, Rose Molly,
   And he killed a sheep about two years old,
   As the dew flies over the green valley.

5. Willie brought it home and laid it on [her] back,
   Jenny go gentle, Rose Molly,
   And with two sticks went whack, whack, whack!
   As the dew flies over the green valley.

182

6. I've sung but not for wealth,
   Jenny go gentle, Rose Molly,
If you want any more you can sing it yourself,
   As the dew flies over the green valley.

80. THE FOOTBOY

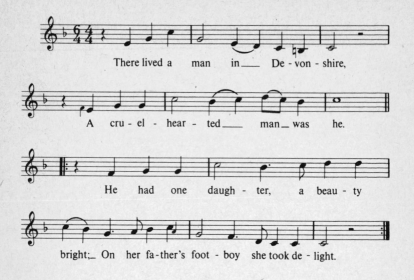

There lived a man in Devonshire,
A cruel-hearted man was he.
He had one daughter, a beauty bright;
On her father's footboy she took delight.

1. There lived a man in Devonshire,
   A cruel-hearted man was he.
        He had one daughter, a beauty bright;
        On her father's footboy she took delight.
        He had one daughter, a beauty bright;
        On her father's footboy she took delight.

2. Oh, one day this couple were left alone,
   And the truth to him she did make known.
        Said he, 'Fair lady, put no trust in me;
        I'm your father's footboy of a low degree.' } 2

3. So this old man in the ambush lay,
   And he heard all that they had to say.
        This made the old man both curse and rage,
        For he knew his daughter was of a tender age. } 2

4. So the very next morning at break of day,
   Said he, 'My lad, you can take your pay.'
        With ready wages he paid him down, } 2
        As the teardrop from his eye did fall.

5. Well he had not got but a mile from town
   When in a circle they did surround.
        They searched his pockets and found within } 2
        A gay gold watch and a diamond ring.

6. So he was taken and lodged in jail,
   No friends or relations to go his bail.
     Great calculations the old man made } 2
     On the executions that he had laid.

7. As he stepped up on the gallows high,
   'O father dear, do you want to see my true love die?
     O father, father, it's a dreadful sight } 2
     For to see my true love all dressed in white.'

8. As she stepped out on the gallows stand
   The old man did not surmise her plan,
     And with a dagger she pierced her heart. } 2
     'Now I welcome death, it to pain and smart.'

9. As she lay in her bloody gore
   Lamenting of her wound so sore,
     'O father, father, you're the worst of men! } 2
     You have brought your daughter to a scornful end.

10. 'So there's just one thing now that I do crave:
    That's to bury us both in the one grave,
      For I love my footboy you know so true,
      And to this *wide world I bid adieu.*'

81. THE HOUSE CARPENTER

1. 'Well met, well met, my own true love,
   And very well met,' said he.
   'I have just returned from the salt, salt sea,
   And it's all for the sake of thee.

2. 'I could have married a queen's daughter,
   And she would have married me,
   But I refused a crown of gold,
   And it's all for the sake of thee.'

3. 'If you could have married a queen's daughter,
   Then she should have married thee,
   For me, young man, you have came too late,
   For I've married a house carpenter.'

4. 'If you will leave your house carpenter
   And go along with me,
   I will take you down where the grass grows green
   On the banks of the River Dee.'

5. 'If I were to leave my house carpenter
   And go along with thee,
   What have you got to maintain a wife
   Or to keep her from slavery?'

6. 'I have seven ships at sea
    And seven more in port,
    And a hundred and twenty-four jolly, jolly boys,
    And they all will wait on thee.'

7. She called then her two pretty babes
    And she kissed them most tenderly,
    Saying, 'Stay at home, my two pretty babes,
    And bear your own father company.'

8. She had not sailed on sea two weeks,
    I'm sure not sailed on three,
    Till here she sat in her new husband's cabin,
    Weeping most bitterly.

9. 'Oh, do you weep for gold?' he said,
    'Or do you weep for fear?
    Or do you weep for your house carpenter
    That you left when you came here?'

10. 'I do not weep for gold,' she said,
    'Nor do I weep for fear,
    But I do weep for my two pretty babes
    That I left when I came here.'

11. She had not sailed on sea three weeks,
    I'm sure not sailed on four,
    Till overboard her fair body she threw,
    And her weeping was heard no more.

12. Her curse did attend a sea sailor's life,
    Her curse did attend a sailor's life,
    For the robbing of a house carpenter,
    And stealing away his wife.

82. THE 'GREEN WILLOW TREE'

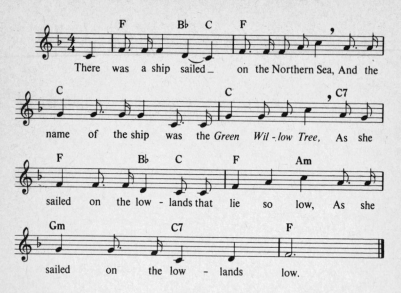

There was a ship sailed _ on the Northern Sea, And the name of the ship was the *Green Wil-low Tree,* As she sailed on the low - lands that lie so low, As she sailed on the low - lands low.

1. There was a ship sailed on the Northern Sea,
   And the name of the ship was the *Green Willow Tree,*
   As she sailed on the lowlands that lie so low,
   As she sailed on the lowlands low.

2. We had not sailed but a league or three
   Till we were overtaken by the *Turkish Revelee,*
   As she sailed on the lowlands that lie so low,
   As she sailed on the lowlands low.

3. Then up spake the cabin boy, saying, 'What will you give me
   If I sink the ship called the *Turkish Revelee?*
   If I sink her in the lowlands that lie so low,
   If I sink her in the lowlands low.'

4. 'I will give you money and I will give you fee,
   And my only daughter I will marry unto thee,
   If you sink her in the lowlands that lie so low,
   If you sink her in the lowlands low.'

5. 'Then wrap me up tight in the black bull-skin
   And throw me overboard, let me sink, die, or swim,
   For I'll sink her in the lowlands that lie so low,
   I will sink her in the lowlands low.'

188

6. So they wrapped him up tight in a black bull-skin
   And threw him overboard, let him sink, die, or swim,
   For he'll sink her in the lowlands that lie so low,
   He will sink her in the lowlands low.

7. So he bent his breast and away swam he,
   For he soon caught up to the *Turkish Revelee*,
   As we sailed her in the lowlands that lie so low,
   As we sailed her on the lowlands low.

8. He had the instruments just for the use,
   And he bored four-and-twenty holes in the bottom of her sluice,
   As she sailed on the lowlands that lie so low,
   As she sailed on the lowlands low.

9. Some were playing cards and some were playing dice:
   They were all taken up in Satan's own advice,
   As he sank her in the lowlands that lie so low,
   As he sank her in the lowlands low.

10. Some ran with hats and some ran with caps,
    All for to stop up the salt water gaps,
    As he sank her in the lowlands that lie so low,
    As he sank her in the lowlands low.

11. Then he bent to his breast and back swam he,
    For he soon caught up to the *Green Willow Tree*,
    As they sailed on the lowlands that lie so low,
    As they sailed on the lowlands low.

12. 'Now throw me a rope and take me on board,
    And prove unto me just as good as your word,
    For I've sank her in the lowlands that lie so low,
    I have sank her in the lowlands sea.'

13. 'I won't throw you a rope nor take you on board,
    Nor prove unto you just as good as my word,
    But I'll sink you in the lowlands that lie so low,
    I will sink you in the lowlands low.'

14. 'If it wasn't for the love that I had for your men,
    I would do unto you as I've done unto them,
    And I'd sink you in the lowlands that lie so low,
    I would sink you in the lowlands low.'

NOTES ON THE SONGS

THE notes below indicate the source of each song from a published collection by the name of the author and the page number; the book title can be found by referring to the Bibliography on page 220. Thus 'Peacock 15' means page 15 of Kenneth Peacock's *Songs of the Newfoundland Outports*. The first page only is given when a song and notes cover more than one page. Different books by the same author are identified by initial letters: thus Creighton MFS refers to Helen Creighton's *Maritime Folk Songs*. The same system is used for references: figures always refer to pages unless otherwise specified.

Unpublished songs from my collection are identified by the name of the singer and the place and date of the recording. If the song has been issued on a commercial record, the company and number are given, and songs from my collection deposited in the National Museum are identified by numbers introduced by FO. British broadside ballads and native North American ballads are identified by the numbers assigned to them in Laws's bibliographical guides. Unless otherwise specified, places named are in Ontario, except for Vancouver which is in British Columbia.

1. *A Fenian Song*
   Fowke and Mills 101
   (Prestige/International 25014)

When Irish nationalists formed the Fenian Brotherhood to fight for independence, they set up branches in North America, and when thousands of Irish-Americans were released from the Union Army after the American Civil War, they decided to form a Fenian army to invade Canada. In the spring of 1866 they assembled along the Niagara frontier and on 31 May about twelve hundred of them crossed the border from Buffalo. The alarm went up in Toronto and the Queen's Own Rifles rushed to the scene under Lieutenant Colonel Alfred Booker. This later famous regiment was then made up largely of college students who impetuously clashed with the Fenians before the other British troops had joined them. As a result they were soundly defeated and retreated in confusion. The Fenians celebrated their victory in this jeering little ditty which Stanley Bâby's father,

a ship captain on the Great Lakes, learned from an Irish sailor who probably took part in the raid.

2. *Bold Wolfe* (A 1)
   Greenleaf 96

The victory and death of General James Wolfe on the Plains of Abraham in 1759 inspired two ballads that have survived to the present: this one, more usually known as *Brave Wolfe*, seems to be known only in North America, and another, *General Wolfe*, or *Bold General Wolfe*, is more common in England (Dean-Smith 58), although it has been sung in Canada (Folkways FM 4005). The North American one was printed in many eighteenth- and nineteenth-century broadsides and songbooks, as Mackenzie shows (198), and was collected from tradition in half a dozen American states as well as in Nova Scotia, Newfoundland and Ontario (Laws NAB 119). Mrs Greenleaf notes: 'This martial and moving song burst on us suddenly in the midst of an evening devoted mainly to the woes of the love-lorn. Its stately measures linger in one's memory with some of its striking lines.' It is interesting that the opening verses were adapted from an old English song, *The Blacksmith* (JFSS VIII 208), which also shares the rather unusual metre.

3. *The Battle of the Windmill*
Fowke and Mills 80

In the early part of the nineteenth century reform parties in Canada began demanding responsible government, but the ruling groups – the Family Compact in Upper Canada and the Château Clique in Lower Canada – stubbornly refused to yield to the requests of the elected assemblies. When the settlers lost hope of constitutional reform, rebellions broke out in 1837, led by William Lyon Mackenzie in Upper Canada and Louis Papineau in Lower Canada. The governments quickly crushed the rebels, but when Mackenzie fled to the United States his American supporters made several raids on Canada throughout 1838. In November some hundred and seventy men crossed the St Lawrence just below Prescott. When they were attacked by a detachment of the Glengarry Militia under Captain George Macdonall and part of the First Grenville Militia under Colonel Richard Duncan Fraser, they withdrew into a large stone windmill. There they held out for four days until a steamboat carrying heavy guns arrived from Kingston and forced their surrender. Eleven were executed, a number imprisoned, and the rest sent to Van Diemen's Land.

Shortly after the battle the Canadian soldiers made up their victory song to the familiar tune of *The Girl I Left behind Me*. In 1942 Ernest Green reported to the Ontario Historical Society:

Along the St Lawrence front the song was sung with great enthusiasm, and many a boy of a hundred years ago had it engraved upon his memory by the oft-repeated rendition of his elders. When the old militiamen of the Johnston and Eastern Districts died out, their sons continued to sing the old song and in turn they passed it on to later generations. So the ditty 'lived on the lips' – if not in the anthologies – and it is still alive in its native habitat.

4. *Un Canadien errant*
Gagnon 81

Although the rebellion of 1837-8 was easily suppressed, the continuing border raids by American sympathizers angered the Tories and provoked harsh treatment of the rebels. Nearly a thousand were imprisoned, scores were transported to Van Diemen's Land, and many of the leaders were hanged. Those who escaped capture had to leave their homes and take refuge in the United States. Their plight inspired a young student, M. A. Gérin-Lajoie, to write *Un Canadien errant*, setting it to the tune of a popular French folk song, *Si tu te mets anguille*. Soon after the song appeared in 1842, French-Canadians were singing it from Acadia on the east coast to the distant reaches of the Northwest Territories.

5. *Moody to the Rescue*
Sung by Patrick Graber, Vancouver, 1970

This is a rare west coast song about events of 1859. In 1856 gold was discovered on the Fraser River and a massive influx of gold-seekers followed. In November 1858 the colony of British Columbia was established and Governor Douglas chose old Fort Langley, or Derby, as its capital. Early in 1859 news reached Derby that there was trouble at Yale on the Fraser River. Ned McGowan, leader of the California miners at Hill's Bar, the main mining area, was said to have broken into the jail and to be heading a conspiracy to overthrow British authority. Despite the midwinter weather and ice-obstructed river, Colonel Richard Clement Moody hurried to Yale with a few Royal Engineers and some marines from a British man-of-war. There he found that the trouble had been greatly exaggerated. A quarrel between two rival magistrates, Whannell and Perrier, over a man accused of assault had led to Whannell arresting Perrier's constable and Perrier issuing a warrant to the miners to arrest Whannell and free the constable. This comic-opera incident became known as 'Ned McGowan's War', although it was completely bloodless.

The background of the song is confused. There may have been verses composed at the time, but the ones Paddy Graber sang seem to have been inspired by the account of the incident in a history, *British Columbia from the Earliest Times to the Present*, by E. O. S. Scholefield and F. W. Howay (Vancouver, 1914). Paddy says he got the verses in 1969 from Henry Hawkins, a ninety-two-year-old patient in Shaughnessy Hospital in Vancouver, who had heard it some fifty years earlier. Although Mr Hawkins could only recite it, Paddy felt it should go to the old Scottish tune of 'The Keach i' the Creel' (Child 281), used also for 'The Overgate', and he seems to have added the '*Ricky doo dum day*' refrain. Another old-timer, Billy Wardell of New Westminster, said he had heard 'old Harry Wiltshire' sing it about 1927, but he did not recognize the refrain, and he claimed the opening line should be 'Word came down to Sappertown.'

6. *By the Hush, me Boys*
Fowke TSSO 52
(Folkways FM 4051)

O. J. Abbott learned this song from Mrs O'Malley, the wife of an Ottawa Valley farmer for whom he worked back in the 1880s. Strangely enough, this American Civil War ballad has not been reported from tradition in the United States. It is an interesting combination of two themes common in many Irish songs: that of emigrating, and of becoming involved in other countries' wars. Thousands of Irish immigrants did 'fight for Lincoln', and the General Mahar mentioned was probably General Thomas Francis Meagher, commander of the famed Irish Brigade that fought at Fredericksburg and Richmond.

7. *An Anti-Confederation Song*
Doyle (1940) 69

In the 1860s the separate British colonies in North America began to discuss a federal union, and in 1867 the Dominion of Canada was established with four provinces: Ontario, Quebec, Nova Scotia and New Brunswick. Delegates from Newfoundland had attended the Quebec Conference at which the federation was planned, but many islanders did not want to give up their separate status. In 1869 a heated election was fought on the issue. Those favouring confederation argued that union would bring lower prices, for high customs duties ran up the cost of everything the Newfoundlanders had to buy. The Anti-Confederates countered by telling the fishermen that Canada would be able to tax their boats and gear, and might even place an export duty on their fish. The campaign was hectic and noisy, and the Anti-Confederates used lively songs to put their arguments across. The result was that the Anti-Confederates elected twenty-one out of thirty candidates, and Newfoundland did not become part of Canada for another eighty years.

8. Chanson de Louis Riel
Cass-Beggs 10
(Folkways FM 4312)

Louis Riel, the leader of the Métis in both the Red River Rebellion of 1870 and the Northwest Rebellion of 1885, was taken prisoner when his followers were defeated at Batoche on 12 May 1885. He was tried, sentenced to death, and hanged in Regina jail on 16 November 1885. Since then his career has inspired books, plays and an opera, and the Saskatchewan Métis still talk and sing of him. Mrs Cass-Beggs got this song from Joseph Gaspard Jeannotte, an old Métis living at Lebret, Saskatchewan. He said that Riel had composed it while in jail, which may well be true for he is known to have written other poems and songs. It appeared first in Mrs Cass-Beggs' *Eight Songs of Saskatchewan* (Toronto, 1963).

9. The 'Flying Cloud' (K 28)
Tom Brandon, Peterborough, 1962
(Folk-Legacy FSC 10)

Dr Laws terms this the best of the pirate ballads, and notes that it is 'unique in its length, its wealth of detail, and its dealing with both slavery and piracy, two colourful blots on human history' (ABBB 11). In *Songs of American Sailormen* Joanna Colcord says it 'dates from the period 1819 to 1823 when the West Indies were finally cleared of pirates by the joint efforts of the United States and several European naval powers' (144).
Although the detailed story seems too vivid not to be based on actual

events, no one has discovered any historical basis for it. No trace of a ship of that name or of a Captain Moore has been found during the era in question. Horace Beck, who wrote an extensive article on 'The Riddle of The "Flying Cloud" ' (JAF 66, 123-33), argues that this was originally two separate ballads of which the one dealing with slavery was the older. If this theory is correct, it is strange that no trace of the separate ballads has been reported.

The 'Flying Cloud' was immensely popular both aboard sailing ships and in the lumber camps. Indeed, Rickaby tells us that 'This is the ballad of which it was said that in order to get a job in the Michigan camps, one had to be able to sing it through from end to end!' (223). All collected versions are remarkably consistent, showing fewer variations than many shorter ballads. It was very well known in Nova Scotia, Newfoundland and Ontario. In addition to the versions Laws lists (ABBB 155), H. P. Beck found it in Maine (247), Leach in Labrador (156), Gale Huntington in Martha's Vineyard (NEF VIII 36), and Peacock in Newfoundland (842). Robert Walker sings it on Folkways FM 4001.

10. The Loss of the 'Ellen Munn'
Mr and Mrs Albert Simms, Toronto, 1960

This is quite a light-hearted treatment of a shipwreck – this time the ship was close enough to land so that no lives were lost. King's Cove and Plate Cove are on the east side of Bonavista Bay; Little Denier is an island at the mouth of Newman Sound on the west side. The area is prone to wrecks: a village on the point is named Salvage. Doyle gave the song in his 1940 booklet (6), but I have found no information about the author or date.

11. *The Banks of Newfoundland*
Fowke TSSO 24
(Folkways FM 4051)

At least half a dozen songs share the title *The Banks of Newfoundland*, but this particular one is rare. Mr Abbott's version is the only one with a tune that has turned up in North America, although there are texts in Eckstorm 219, Gordon MSS No. 1805, and McGinnis MSS No. 26. It does not seem to be known in England or Scotland, but Joseph Ransom gives it in *Songs of the Wexford Coast* (18) and Sam Henry (No. 569) has another Irish version.

The story is typical of many ballads about shipwrecks on the Atlantic crossing: the sailing ships that carried immigrants were usually overcrowded and many of them were old and unseaworthy. The drawing of lots to see who will be killed to feed the rest is a fairly common motif in old sea ballads.

12. *The Ryans and the Pittmans*
Doyle (1940) 53

This rollicking tale of a young fisherman's love affairs is a Newfoundland offshoot of the widely known English capstan shanty *Spanish Ladies*, which described the headlands sighted in a homeward voyage through the English Channel. Pacific whalemen later remade it to tell of the *Talcahuano Girls*, with a chorus: 'We'll rant and we'll roar like true Huasco whalermen,' and Australian drovers sang their farewell to the *Brisbane Ladies*. The Newfoundland version has borrowed verses 2, 8, 9 and 10 from the whalers' song; the remaining verses about Bob Pittman and his courtship were composed around 1875 by W. H. Le-Messurier who was editor of the *Evening Herald* and later deputy minister of customs in St John's.

James Murphy printed it in *Old Songs of Newfoundland* in 1912; it appeared in all the Doyle booklets; and Mrs Greenleaf heard it from Mr Le-Messurier himself, and also from Tom White of Sandy Cove, whose version had acquired some variations (266). Paradise, Oderin, Presque, Brule and St Kyran's are tiny fishing villages along the west coast of Placentia Bay.

13. *The Petty Harbour Bait Skiff*
Doyle (1940) 28

Newfoundlanders sing literally scores of songs about shipwrecks: Peacock gives thirty-two different 'Tragic Sea Ballads', and there are many others. One of the most popular is this account of the disaster that struck a small fishing vessel in 1852. Mr C. R. Vincent of the Public Archives of Canada sent me this account from a St John's paper, *The Newfoundlander*, of 10 June 1852:

We much regret to announce that during the gale of Monday last Mr French and five hands were lost in a bait-skiff outside Petty Harbour. They had just returned from Conception Bay with a load of bait, when, nearly at the entrance to the harbour a sudden squall took the skiff. She appears to have gone down stern foremost – the solitary survivor of the crew having clung to the jib-boom which remained over water; in which perilous situation the poor fellow was found and rescued by the crew of another boat.

The ballad is credited to John Grace, a Newfoundland sailor and bard who later died in Brazil. The flowery language and internal rhymes indicate that he was thoroughly steeped in Irish balladry. James Murphy, who printed the text in *Old Songs of Newfoundland* in 1912, noted that 'A man named Menchington was the only one who was saved.'

As this song should go at a rather slow pace, it is usually shortened by omitting certain verses and combining others. The verses usually omitted are 2, 7, 9, 10 and 11.

14. The Wreck of the 'Mary Summers'
Charles Cates, Vancouver, 1960

Where the Petty Harbour bait skiff and the *Ellen Munn* were small local vessels, the *Mary Summers* was an ocean-going freighter. Captain Cates, who learned the song from his father, an east coast seaman, spoke of it as a Nova Scotia ship, but there is no record of it in Canadian or British shipping registers. The port from which it sailed, St Andrews, is on the New Brunswick coast. The ballad gives a very realistic account of the difficulties a sailing ship could meet on an ocean passage: many such ships were lost with all hands, but this time the crew was lucky.

15. The Old 'Polina'
Doyle (1955) 44

Gerald Doyle got this lively whaling song from Captain Peter Carter and Harry R. Burton of Greenspond, Bonavista Bay. It gives a vivid and accurate account of the race that took place each spring when the whaling ships set out from Dundee 'on a western ocean passage' heading for St John's. C. R. Vincent of the Public Archives of Canada notes:

Early in the new year some of the Dundee whalers set out for Newfoundland to participate in the Newfoundland seal fishery. They would sign on Newfoundland hunters in early March, take part in the sealing, discharge the seal pelts and Newfoundlanders back in St John's in April, and sail north to Green-

land waters for the whaling, arriving back in Dundee in the early fall. On the outward passage from Dundee to St John's, despite the usually bad weather, there was considerable competition between the ships as to which could make the fastest trip, both for the sake of the ship's reputation and because the first ships in St John's were better able to get a good crew of seal hunters.

He says that the *Polina*, or *Polynia*, launched in 1861 from the yard of Alexander Stephen & Sons, was a 472-ton vessel owned by the Dundee Seal and Whale Fishing Company. It was commanded by Captain William Guy from 1883 until it was lost in Davis Strait on 10 July 1891, being crushed between two ice floes in a gale. Three of the other ships mentioned – *Arctic*, *Aurora* and *Terra Nova* – were well known Dundee whalers. The passage mentioned in the song was probably in early 1891 when the *Polynia* was damaged in a gale on the way to Newfoundland.

The same song is known in Britain as *The 'Balaena'*, which seems to be the result of confusion between two like-sounding names. A. L. Lloyd notes: 'In 1893 the *Balaena* reported plenty of finn whales down in southern ice' (leaflet for Topic 12T174), so they were obviously two different ships. However, it appears that the song was originally composed about the *Polynia* rather than the *Balaena* because the British version retains the name of Captain Guy.

16. The Ferryland Sealer
Peacock 120

Kenneth Peacock notes that this detailed description of a sealing voyage 'is one of the best of the native ballads to come out of Newfoundland'. It is almost too vivid an account of the hunt. The baby seals are born in February, and about 20 March ships head out from Newfoundland ports for the ice floes along the coast of Labrador. When the men sight the seals they land on the ice and hunt them with gaffs – long sticks with iron hooks on the end – or shoot them with rifles. In recent years the slaughter has come in for much criticism, and it is now carefully supervised to prevent unnecessary cruelty.

The ballad dates back over a century: Mrs Eckstorm gives a text she got from a Prince Edward Island captain who learned it in the 1860s (324). Ferryland is a small village on the east coast of the Avalon Peninsula south of St John's, and Cape Broyle is just north of it.

17. Hard, Hard Times
Paul Emberley, Bay de Verde, Nfld, 1954

The great depression of the 1930s fell especially hard on Newfoundland fishermen: the collapse of international markets made it difficult to sell their fish at any price. For years many of them had to live on the government dole of six cents a day: a plight reflected in several songs. This one, which William James Emberley of Bay de Verde adapted from an older song, has proved remarkably durable. The version given here, which Don Brittain of the National Film Board recorded from Mr Emberley's son, is probably close to the original. Peacock collected two versions with different tunes (57), one of which Doyle included in his 1955 songbook (28). It is interesting to note that the song has already acquired two additional verses – about the baker and the parson – indicating its close relationship to what Archie Green terms 'the multi-branched tree *Hard Times* whose roots go to a

family of English eighteenth-century satiric broadsides. One British form of this piece which ridiculed various callings was titled *Chapter of Cheats: Or, the Roguery of All Trades*' (leaflet for Folkways FH 5273). For American versions see Gardner 443 and Lomax 103. Incidentally, 'kentle' in verse 3 is an obsolete form for quintal, a hundredweight.

18. Taking Gair in the Night
Fowke TSSO 150

Albert Simms, a former Newfoundlander now living in Toronto, learned this local Newfoundland song in his home in McCallum Harbour about 1928. He knew Jerry Fudge, the man who made it up: he was then a young fisherman of about twenty-two. Some thirty years later Kenneth Peacock found a shorter version of it in Rose Blanche (145). The 'gair' of the title means gear – the trawls used in fishing for capelin. Penguin Island, the locale of the fishing banks, is nine miles south of Cape La Hune on the south coast of Newfoundland between Fortune Bay and Port aux Basques. The catalogue of fishermen and their boats is typical of many east coast songs, and the description of the fishermen's life follows the traditional pattern of many older songs about the hardships of those who go down to the sea in ships.

19. Farewell to Nova Scotia
Creighton TSNS 265

This has become the best known of all Nova Scotia songs, partly because the Halifax CBC television show, 'Sing-along Jubilee', used it as a theme, and Catherine McKinnon recorded it. Helen Creighton collected it in the 1930s from half a dozen singers in the Petpeswick and Chezzetcook districts, some twenty-five miles east of Halifax: they told her that it was formerly sung in the schools. Mrs Carrie Grover learned it when she was a little girl in Nova Scotia as *Adieu to Nova Scotia* (208), and Marius Barbeau found another version in Beauce County, Quebec, as *On the Banks of Jeddore* (CAS 1). The tune is similar to one Cecil Sharp gives for *The Lowlands Low*.

20. Hogan's Lake
Fowke LSNW 37
(Folkways FM 4052)

These verses, which Mr Abbott learned in a lumber camp in the Ottawa Valley about 1890, are a specialized form of the widespread *Lumber Camp Song* (Greenleaf 321) which was sung in practically every camp in the northeastern states and eastern Canada under varying titles. Originally it was a loose adaptation of the English music-hall song *Jim the Carter Lad*, with versions called *Jack the Shanty Lad* or *The Jolly Shanty Lad* (LSNW 34), but gradually it became fully naturalized, as in this account of a square-timber camp. In the early days the hewers sliced off the four sides of the huge pine trunks to make square timber which could be loaded on ships without waste space. Because this wasted nearly a quarter of the wood, the square-timber camps gradually gave way to logging camps in which the trees were sawed into twelve- or sixteen-foot lengths.

The tune used for this whole group of lumbering songs also serves for the Great Lakes ballad, *The Trip of the Bigler* (Folkways FM 4018), and for an English fishing song, *The Dogger Bank* (Folkways FG 3597).

21. The Lake of the Caogama
Fowke LSNW 87

This lively little shanty song comes from a lumber camp on the northern shore of the Ottawa River. Lake Caogama (pronounced keg-a-ma) is some eighty miles north of Arnprior. These particular verses are not widely known – I got them only from Lennox Gavan of Quyon, Quebec – but they are typical of many shantyboy complaint songs, and they go to an attractive old Irish tune: one that Patrick Joyce noted in 1853 and to which he set his song of *The Leprehaun* (AIM 100).

22. How We Got Up to the Woods Last Year
O. J. Abbot, Hull, Quebec, 1958
(Folkways FM 4052)

This song from the northern Ontario woods tells how the shantyboys made their way into the lumber camps back in the 1880s before a railway was built in that region. It was widely known in Ontario, and other versions give a more detailed account of the trip from Arnprior, some thirty miles west of Ottawa, through Renfrew and Dacre to Lake Opeongo in Algonquin Park, a distance of about a hundred miles. Migrant shantyboys carried the ditty down to the Michigan camps where E. C. Beck heard it as *Drunk on the Way* (414). He terms it a 'moniker' song because it gives the names of the boys in the gang, and Mr Abbott kept up the tradition by adding the names of Albert Tapp and Jack McCann, two men with whom he had worked and from whom he had learned songs. I suspect he added the line, 'We all joined in a good sing-song', for it does not appear elsewhere. Two other Canadian versions are in *Lumbering Songs from the Northern Woods*, 162.

23. Dans les chantiers
Gagnon 100

This is one of the oldest French-Canadian lumbering songs: it was first noted by a nineteenth-century French-Canadian writer, J. C. Taché, in *Les Soirées Canadiennes* in 1863. Gagnon gives two slightly different versions and describes how the '*bucherons canadiens*' raced over the icy fields on snowshoes singing this song. He explains that in France the word '*chantier*' means a workshop, but in Canada it is used both generally for the lumber camp as a whole, and specifically for the log houses in which the men live. From it came the word 'shanty' for the buildings and the name 'shantyboys'.

24. The Jones Boys
Manny 124

This little ditty was the favourite song of Lord Beaverbrook, the British newspaper baron who grew up in the lumbering district of Miramichi in New Brunswick. When he gave quarter-hour chimes to the University of New Brunswick, he arranged for them to play this tune.

The verse commemorates James and John Jones, the sons of a Cornish-born immigrant who built a grist mill on a brook flowing into the Nor-West Miramichi in the 1840s. When he died in 1866 James took over the grist mill and John a saw-mill near by. Nick Underhill sings a longer song describing the brothers' problems on Folkways FM 4053.

This single verse is widely known in the Maritimes, and Alan Mills got a second from Louise Manny which he sings on Folkways FW 8744:

Oh, the Jones boys!
They built a still on the top of a hill,
And they worked one night, and they worked one day,
And Lord! – how that little old still did pay!

25. Jimmy Whelan (C 7)
Fowke LSNW 111
(Folkways FM 4052)

Accidents in which shantyboys were drowned on river drives were all too common: one informant said there were twenty-seven crosses beside one rapid near Pembroke. Such tragedies inspired a number of ballads, of which *The Jam on Gerry's Rocks* (C 1) is the best known. The facts behind it are elusive, but Jimmy Whelan – actually James Phalen – was killed on Ontario's Mississippi River, a tributary of the Ottawa. Rickaby gives 1878 as the date; James Phalen's grandniece, Mary C. Phelan of Ottawa, thinks it was 1876, and she names Timothy Doyle as the ballad's composer. Laws lists versions from Michigan, Wisconsin, Minnesota, Maine and New Brunswick (NAB 150); Shoemaker found it in Pennsylvania (86); and Vincent gives a west coast version (39).

26. Lost Jimmy Whelan (C 8)
Fowke LSNW 114 (FO 4-39)

This lament inspired by the death of Jimmy Whelan was widely sung in Ontario, and it spread throughout the Maritime Provinces, Michigan, Maine and Wisconsin. In addition to the versions Laws lists (NAB 150), Manny found it in New Brunswick (263), and Peacock in Newfoundland (385). Robert Walker and Mary Dumphy sing traditional versions on Folkways FM 4001 and FE 4075.

This ballad is almost certainly adapted from an older British one: *The Blantyre Explosion* in A. L. Lloyd's *Come All Ye Bold Miners* (129) is a relative, but the ancestor has not been identified. The tune is one commonly used for *The Lass of Glenshee*.

27. *Peter Emberley* (C 27)
   Manny 160
   (Tune: Folkways FM 4053)

This tale of the young man from Prince Edward Island who was fatally injured in the Miramichi woods when a log rolled on him is the favourite ballad of New Brunswick. John Calhoun, one of the men who drove the injured lad down to his employer's home, described his fate in these verses, and a local singer, Abraham Munn, set them to an old Irish tune that has served for many songs both in Ireland and North America. As winter conditions made it impossible for a priest to conduct Emberley's funeral, someone added a verse asking that his grave be blessed, and most singers adopted it, much to Calhoun's annoyance. Louise Manny gives the nine verses Calhoun wrote; the extra verse is at the end. Nearly all singers omit verses 4 and 9, and many sing only 1, 2, 5, 6, 7 and the added verse: for example, Marie Hare on Folk-Legacy FSC 9, and Wilmot MacDonald on Folkways FM 4053, whose tune is used here. The song is well known along the east coast: Laws lists versions from Maine, New Hampshire, Nova Scotia, New Brunswick and New-foundland (NAB 160); and it has also spread to Ontario (Fowke LSNW 127).

28. *When the Shantyboy Comes Down*
   Fowke LSNW 159
   (Folkways FM 4052)

Just as sailors go on a spree when they reach shore after a long voyage, so the shantyboys whoop it up when they reach town after a long winter in the woods. It was natural for the British sailors' song *Jack Tar on Shore* (K 39) to be adapted to describe *The Lumberman in Town*, as this ballad is known on the east coast. Mrs Eckstorm, who gives the earliest text (96), comments: 'This is one of the finest of the old woods songs and if nothing else showed that it came from the British provinces we might guess it from the melancholia in it; this self-pity is not a characteristic of the native of Maine.' The song is fairly rare: in addition to Mrs Eckstorm's text from 1901, there is a text in the Gordon MSS (No. 263); Ives got two versions from a Prince Edward Island singer (NEF 2, 58; 5, 68), and Vincent includes it in his *Lumberjack Songs* (4).

29. *The Scarborough Settler's Lament*
   Fowke and Mills 94

Although most Canadian songs are Irish-oriented, Scotland also provided many of our early settlers. Some left the Highlands after the Jacobite Rebellions, and more followed when sheep enclosures drove small farmers from their land. They settled in Cape Breton, Nova Scotia, and in Glengarry, Perth, Dundas and Scarborough townships in Ontario. Many of them were homesick for their native land, and Sandy Glendenning, who settled in Scarborough (now part of Metropolitan Toronto) in 1840, described his feelings in these verses, setting them to the first part of the old Scots air, *Of A' the Airts the Wind Can Blaw*. The song had some currency throughout Ontario, elsewhere being called simply *A Scottish Settler's Lament*. Sheila Bucher, longtime editor of the 'Old Favourites' page in the *Family Herald*, says her grandmother sang it to the tune of *The Irish Emigrant's Lament*.

30. *The Backwoodsman* (C 1)
Emerson Woodcock, Peterborough,
1957
(Folkways FM 4052)

This tale of a country boy's night out
has a surprising vitality. It sounds like
a local ballad – Omemee and Downeyville are small towns near Peterborough
– but it is actually one of the most
widespread North American songs,
having been sung in at least eight
states and three provinces. It seems
to have started in Vermont early in the
nineteenth century and spread out
from there. The titles vary: *The Green
Mountain Boys*, *The Cordwood Cutter*,
I Came to This Country, *The Wood
Hauler*, and *One 'Lection Morning*, and
the place names are always localized,
but the incidents and phrasing have
remained remarkably constant in
widely separated regions over more
than a century. Mr Woodcock's version is a little shorter than most: for
a longer Ontario version and references
see Fowke LSNW 173.

31. *The Honest Working Man*
Tune: Patrick Graber, Vancouver,
1970
Text: McCawley 7

Stuart McCawley, who published his
small booklet, *Cape Breton Come-All-
Ye*, in 1929, noted that this 'was the
national anthem of the Cape Breton
workers many years ago, and a popular
song with the troops in World War I.
It was written as a piece of irony aimed
at the importation of surplus labour
in the summer months. Anyone not
"porridge-bred" and Gaelic was a
"foreigner".' It was still popular after
the war, for Paddy Graber's uncle, Jim
Meade, heard it when he spent some
time in Canada in the 1920s, and
Paddy remembers the first verse he
sang. Its tune is Irish: the Graber

family used it for a Tipperary song,
The Hills of Mallabawn, which dates
back to the eighteenth century.
Alphonse MacDonald who compiled
The Cape Breton Songster in 1935 gives
The Honest Working Man as 'Cape
Breton's national anthem', and both
Helen Creighton and Margaret Sargent
have collected it from tradition.

32. *L'Habitant d' Saint-Barbe*
Mills 48

This little cumulative song is known in
various forms among the French-
Canadians of both Quebec and the
Maritimes. The Montreal folksinger
Alan Mills learned this version from a
Cape Breton fisherman named Peter
Chiasson in a little fishing village near
Cheticamp, Nova Scotia, in the sum-
mer of 1954. Unlike most cumulative
songs which add phrases at the end,
this has its cumulative section at the
beginning of each verse. A very similar
English song, *The Wild Man of
Borneo*, is also known in Nova Scotia
(Creighton TSNS 258).

33. *Life in a Prairie Shack*
Fowke and Johnston MFSC 109

Old-timers loved to make fun of the
greenhorn or tenderfoot when he
showed up in the Canadian west, just
as Australian sheep-shearers used to
ridicule the 'new chums' out from
England. The tenderfoot was often a
remittance man – the black sheep of an
upper-class English family who was
shipped out to the colonies when he got
into trouble at home. This little ditty
indicates how hard it was for such
tenderly reared men to adjust to the
hard life of the prairies. Captain
Charles Cates got it from his father
who had worked in the Canadian west
in the 1880s. It goes to the familiar
tune of *Life on the Ocean Wave*. John

Lomax heard a similar song as *Life in a Half-Breed Shack* (386).

34. *The Alberta Homesteader*
Fowke and Mills 144

After the Canadian government took over Rupert's Land from the Hudson's Bay Company in 1869 it encouraged settlement by offering a quarter section free to anyone who would live on it for three years. This brought a great influx of men from Britain and eastern Canada, but to many the free land proved a mixed blessing. There were few trees on the prairies so most homesteads were built out of the tough prairie sod. Food was scarce and the weather was bad: drought and dust storms in summer, frost and blizzards in winter. There were grasshopper plagues and prairie fires, and day after day the wind blew relentlessly across the flat plains. Not surprisingly, many homesteaders decided that living there for three years was too high a price to pay for their farm. The tougher ones who stuck it out liked to describe the hardships in songs like this. Some Albertan adapted it from an American pioneer song usually known as *The Greer County Bachelor* (Lomax 282). It usually goes to the tune of *The Irish Washerwoman*, although it was also sung to *Villikens and His Dinah*.

35. *The Kelligrews Soiree*
Doyle (1940) 16

This lively description of a high-spirited party is one of the most popular land songs of Newfoundland. The words were written by one of the Island's favourite bards, John Burke, who used to sponsor variety shows in St John's until his death in 1925. He patterned his ditty on Irish music-hall songs like *The Irish Jubilee* and *Lanigan's Ball*, and set it to a rollicking

tune. Kelligrews is a small village on the east coast of Conception Bay west of St John's, and *Clara Nolan's Ball* was the title of an American vaudeville song of the nineteenth century.

36. *Bachelor's Hall*
Peacock 237

This is the Newfoundland version of a fairly widespread song about the everlasting war between the sexes. Sharp gives three Appalachian versions as *When Boys Go A-Courting* (II 205), and Gardner (441) and Fuson (133) have it as *Bachelor's Hall*.

37. *Feller from Fortune*
Peacock 55

Another rollicking dance song that reflects the life in Newfoundland's outports, this is set to an old Irish fiddle tune used in the United States for the college song *Co-ca-che-lunk*. Bonavista is one of the largest ports on the east coast, Carbonear is the largest town in Conception Bay, west of St John's, and Fortune is a fishing settlement on the Burin Peninsula on the south coast. Cassis is a wine imported from the tiny French island of St Pierre off Newfoundland's south coast.

38. *Duffy's Hotel*
Manny 76

This account of the riotous doings in Boiestown on the Miramichi River is one of the best known songs in New Brunswick. It was apparently made up by several local inhabitants some eighty years ago. Duffy's Hotel used to be across from the Boiestown railway station. W. M. Doerflinger, who gave a slightly different version in *Shantymen and Shantyboys* (268), notes that Delaney was a lumberwoods teamster and that the Mansion was a haunt of the loggers on their way down-river. The tune is Irish, used for such songs as *A Trip Over the Mountain*, *A Damsel Possessed of Great Beauty* and *Caroline and Her Young Sailor Bold*. It also serves for a well known Newfoundland lumbering song, *The Badger Drive* (Doyle, 1940, 29).

39. *Alouette!*

This is by far the best known of all Canadian songs: it has long been used by both French and English Canadians for community singing. At numerous social gatherings even those who know no other word of French can be heard chanting lustily: '*Alouette, gentille alouette, alouette, je t'y plumerai.*' Some may not realize that they are singing a somewhat peculiar ode to a skylark in which the lark is informed that 'I will pluck your head, your beak, your nose, your eyes, your neck, your wings, your back, your feet, your tail . . .'. In 1917 the veteran collector E. Z. Massicotte noted: 'Few folk songs are as well known today as *Alouette*. I find it, for the first time, in my old notebook of 1883 . . .'. In *Jongleur Songs of Old Quebec* Barbeau notes that 'This rigmarole was not so popular formerly as it is today,' and cites a number of variants (189).

40. *Ah! Si mon moine voulait danser!*
Gagnon 129

Today this is one of the best known French-Canadian songs, but it was not widespread in tradition. In *Alouette* (170) Barbeau notes that it was collected only three times: its popularity results from its use by the singer Charles Marchand and his Troubadours de Bytown.

In France the word '*moine*' means 'monk' but in Quebec it also means

'top', so children sometimes sang it as they twirled their tops. The French text tells of a young girl who offers a monk various gifts to induce him to dance: a hood, a sash, a rosary, a homespun gown and a psalter, and concludes: 'If he hadn't taken a vow of poverty, I'd give him many other things.' The English words shift the emphasis to a young man coaxing a girl to dance.

41. *En roulant ma boule*
Gagnon 12

So popular is this old French tale of the prince who shoots a duck that Barbeau compiled ninety-two versions of *Trois beaux canards* for *Les Archives de Folklore* of Laval University (II 97) in 1947, and added fifteen more in *Jongleur Songs of Old Quebec* (97). He notes that the same text is preserved in all versions, but that no less than thirty or forty different songs with distinct tunes and refrains have been made from it. Originally a French *jongleur* song of the fifteenth century, it became the favourite paddling song of the *voyageurs*. The form given here is the best known, with *V'la l'bon vent* second in popularity.

42. *D'où viens-tu, bergère?*
Gagnon 266

This old French carol embodies the legend of a shepherdess who visited the stable in Bethlehem on the first Christmas night. Gagnon says that it was never sung in church but was very popular in French-Canadian homes. It came to Canada with the early settlers in the seventeenth century and has continued to be sung ever since.

43. I'se the B'y that Builds the Boat
Fowke and Johnston FSC 116

This typical dance ditty is one of Newfoundland's best known songs. Dr Leslie Bell heard it there some twenty years ago and the Leslie Bell Singers recorded it. His version appeared in *Folk Songs of Canada* in 1954 and Doyle included it in his 1955 songbook. Peacock, who noted it from two St John's singers (64), explains that a 'flake is a platform covered with pieces of bark (rings) on which the filleted cod are spread to dry out'.

44. Who'll be King but Charlie?
Mrs A. Fraser, Lancaster, 1961

This fragment of a fairly well known Scottish song is interesting because it serves as a link between the Jacobite song and the many American verses usually identified as *Weevily Wheat*. (For references, Brown III 100.) Charlie was of course Bonny Prince Charlie, the hero of many Scottish songs. He and his seven companions landed at Moidart on 25 July 1745; hence the title by which the original song is sometimes known, *The News from Moidart Cam' Yestreen*. It has been attributed to Lady Caroline Nairne. The original had five stanzas telling how the Highlanders rallied to support their prince, with a chorus roughly corresponding to Mrs Fraser's, except that 'Around him fling your royal king' is a corruption of 'Around him cling wi' a' your kin'. With this she combines the 'Charlie likes to kiss the girls' stanza found in most versions of the widespread play-party song. Creighton found a similar verse in Nova Scotia (MFS 125). Both forms were known in Kentucky: see *Folk-Songs of the Southern United States* by Josiah H. Combs, edited by D. K. Wilgus, 235, note 299.

45. Vive la Canadienne!
Gagnon 4

This lively toast to the Canadian girl has rarely been collected from tradition, but it has become very popular in recent times. Barbeau, who gives a longer version in *Alouette!* (35), notes that it is both Canadian, because its words were composed in the Laurentians, and French, because its inspiration and melody came from the mother country in the seventeenth century. He says the old French song *Par derrièr' chez mon père*, also known as *Vole, mon cœur, vole*, is one of the finest in the repertoire of France and French Canada: it was very popular with the *voyageurs*, one of whom probably composed the new words.

46. The Star of Belle Isle
Peacock 598

This ode to a fair maiden is one of Newfoundland's loveliest songs. The text appeared in the first Doyle songbook in 1927; Mrs Greenleaf collected a tune in 1929 at Fleur de Lys, 125 miles south of Belle Isle; and Peacock found it in 1952 at King's Cove, some 170 miles to the south-east. It seems to be a local adaptation of an old Irish love song, *Loch Erin's Sweet Riverside*, and also resembles another Irish song, *The Lass of Dunmore*, both of which Francis Bennett of Quyon, Quebec, sang to the same tune. Another native Newfoundland song, *The Green Shores of Fogo*, also uses the same fine Mixolydian tune (Peacock 522).

47. The Star of Logy Bay
Doyle (1955) 59

The plot here is similar to that of many British ballads in which parents object to their daughter's choice, but this seems to be a native composition rather than a local version of an older ballad. The author is not known, but the song is very popular in Newfoundland where it is sung to several different tunes: Doyle gives another in his 1940 edition, and Mrs Greenleaf found a third (270). Logy Bay and Torbay are small towns north of St John's.

48. *Mary Ann*
Barbeau CAS 41

This is a Canadian version of a British broadside ballad that was printed in W. Henderson's *Victorian Street Ballads* as *My Mary Ann*. Dr Barbeau heard it in 1920 in Tadoussac, Quebec, from Edouard Hovington, a former Hudson's Bay trapper, then about ninety, who had learned it from an Irish sailor around 1850. His version has become very well known through numerous reprintings and recordings. It is related to *The True Lover's Farewell:* for references see Cox 413.

49. *C'est l'aviron*
Fowke and Johnston FSC 58

Like so many French-Canadian songs, this was transplanted from medieval France and, with an added refrain, became a favourite of the *voyageurs* paddling along Canada's endless rivers. As one early traveller in Canada noted: 'Their song is like the murmur of the river itself. It seems endless. After each short line comes the refrain, and the story twines itself along like a slender creeping plant.' Barbeau, who gives it with a different tune in *Jongleur Songs of Old Quebec* (138), compares its story to that of *The Baffled Knight* (Child 112), and lists other Canadian references. The version given here, which is the best known, was collected by E. Z. Massicote in 1927.

50. *The 'H'Emmer Jane'*
Clyde Gilmour, Toronto, 1957

This lachrymose lament goes to the ubiquitous tune of *Villikens and His Dinah*, used for several Newfoundland songs, and, like that more famous ballad, it satirizes the broadsides which told such heart-rending stories in all seriousness. No one seems to know who is responsible for the tearful tale, but it is much beloved in Newfoundland. A broadside set at the Golden Hind Press in Madison, N.J., in 1941 gives a text as sung by Eric Penny and claims: '*Emmer Jane* is a folk song from the south shore of Newfoundland, here printed for the first time.' A version from C. M. Lane of St John's appears in *More Folk Songs of Canada* (156), and a version from Bob Mac-Leod is in the 1966 Doyle songbook (49).

In a letter (11 September 1972) Mr MacLeod writes: 'I first heard it sung by a man in an Indian Bay lumbering camp during a visit there about 1939 or 1940 when I was helping the late Gerald S. Doyle to collect songs for his Newfoundland song book .... I used it many times in Newfoundland programmes I did for entertainment at convention gatherings both here at home and in the Maritimes. Probably as a result of this it did become more well known.'

Clyde Gilmour learned it from Mr MacLeod when he was stationed in St John's during the Second World War, and his version has acquired a few variations. It is always sung with an exaggerated Newfoundland accent.

51. *The Jolly Raftsman O*
Fowke TSSO 78 (Prestige/ International 25014)

This is another unusual song from Mrs Fraser. She learned it from her mother who in her turn probably learned it from her father who had worked in the lumber woods. I have found no other trace of this little love lyric: I think the tune is Gaelic, but have been unable to pin it down.

52. The Red River Valley
Mrs A. Fraser, Lancaster, 1961

This is probably the best known folk song on the Canadian prairies. It is also widely known in the United States, where it was believed to be a Texas adaptation of an 1896 popular song, *In the Bright Mohawk Valley*. Later research indicates that it was known in at least five Canadian provinces before 1896, and was probably composed during the Red River Rebellion of 1870 ('*The Red River Valley* Re-Examined', *Western Folklore*, 23, 163). Later versions are short and generalized, but the early form told of an Indian or half-breed girl lamenting the departure of her white lover, a soldier who came west with Colonel Wolseley to suppress the first Riel rebellion. Mrs Fraser's text is very similar to the earliest known versions, and Barbeau gives another traditional version from Calgary in *Come A-Singing* (7).

53. The Young Spanish Lass
Fowke TSSO 148

This ballad, from Albert Simms, a former Newfoundlander, is a neat adaptation of the story told in the popular American ballad, *The Little Mohea* (H 8), and the English broadside, *The Indian Lass* (Mackenzie 154). Certain phrases show that it is descended from *The Indian Lass* rather than from *The Little Mohea*, but it has a definite Newfoundland slant: Newfoundland sailors often visited Spain where they took shiploads of dried codfish, returning with cargoes of molasses and salt.

54. Young MacDonald
Mrs A. Fraser, Lancaster, 1962

This macaronic song with its mixture of English and Gaelic is obviously derived from an old Gaelic wauking or milling song, but I have failed to identify the original. The English words suggest that it is partly a translation of the original Gaelic verses combined with a local reference to the 'young MacDonald' who was 'brought up here in Glengarry' and is 'off to Colorado'. The first two stanzas have the quality of traditional Scottish love lyrics; the third has the more prosaic tone of a local song. The original Gaelic chorus and phrases at the end of each stanza have become too garbled to be translated. Mrs Fraser learned the song from her brother-in-law, Mr John A. MacDonald, who learned it some forty years earlier. Mrs Fraser says that she heard her mother mention a man known as John (the Farmer) MacDonald who went out to Leadville, Colorado, towards the end of the last century. MacDonald is one of the commonest names in Ontario's Glengarry county.

55. À la claire fontaine
Gagnon 1

In 1865 Ernest Gagnon, the first important collector of French-Canadian songs, wrote: '*Depuis le petit enfant de sept ans jusqu'au vieillard aux cheveux blancs, tout le monde, en Canada, sait et chante la "Claire Fontaine". On n'est pas canadien sans cela.*' It has been the most popular song of French Canadians ever since Champlain's men sang it at Port-Royal in 1608 when they formed L'Ordre de

Bon Temps. The *coureurs-de-bois*, explorers and fur traders used it as a paddling song, and the *habitants* and their wives sang it as they cleared their farms along the St Lawrence. Ever since it has been the unofficial anthem of French Canada. It came originally from France where it was composed by a medieval *jongleur*, and literally dozens of versions have been noted in Canada. Barbeau lists a dozen in print and thirty-six in manuscript in *Jongleur Songs of Old Quebec* (91).

56. *Harbour Le Cou*
Peacock 198

This amusing ditty was not widely known in 1951 when Kenneth Peacock collected it from Bill Brennan of Stock Cove, who had learned it in a local lumber camp. Then Doyle printed it in his 1955 booklet (26) and many outport singers learned it from the booklet or from local radio programmes. Harbour Le Cou is a small fishing village on the southwest coast of Newfoundland near Port aux Basques, and Torbay is north of St John's.

57. *The Lonesome Scenes of Winter* (H 12)
John Leahy, Douro, 1958
(Prestige/International 25018)

Although it resembles several British ballads about girls who scorn their suitors, this form has been found only in North America. It is fairly widespread, turning up not only in Nova Scotia and Ontario but in half a dozen states (Laws NAB 236). It was particularly popular in Nova Scotia where Helen Creighton collected four versions (TSNS 209), and Carrie Grover gives another (152). In them the rejected suitor says he'll head for Flanders to forget the girl, but Mr Leahy's version is more general.

Helen Creighton also found it in New Brunswick (FSNB 112); Kenneth Peacock reports it from Newfoundland (445); and J. F. Doering found it in Indiana under the title of 'The Lover's Lament' (JAF 57, 73).

58. *The False Young Man*
Barbeau CAS 49

This song about disappointed love has turned up in many places under many titles. Cecil Sharp, who named it *The False Young Man*, found ten versions in the Appalachians (II 51); Korson found it in Pennsylvania as *The Cottage Door* (29); and Mrs Grover knew it in Nova Scotia as *The Lover Proved False* (27). In England Vaughan Williams calls it *As I Walked Out* (JFSS II 152), and in Ireland Hughes gives it as *The Verdant Braes o' Skreen* (I 1) and Sam Henry as *My Love John* (No. 593). In Canada it became widely known when Montreal folksingers Alan Mills and Hélène Baillargeon used it as the theme of their CBC radio series 'Songs de Chez Nous'. (For another Canadian version and further references see TSSO 42 and 169.)

59. *Down by Sally's Garden*
Leo Spencer, Lakefield, 1957

This is a good song in its own right, but it is probably of most interest because it inspired W. B. Yeats' more famous *Down by the Sally Gardens*. The *Feis Ceoil Collection of Irish Airs* by A. Darley and P. J. McCall, published in Dublin in 1914, gives a version with this note: 'From MS. of Mr James Cogley, Duffrey Hill, Enniscorthy. This song is well known in South Leinster. Mr W. B. Yeats has rewritten it' (14, 43). In *Victorian*

Street Ballads (16) W. Henderson writes: 'It is pleasing to note that in at least one instance a poet of high standing did not disdain to take a hint from a street ballad. One of the six stanzas of *The Rambling Boys of Pleasure* – a poorish production – runs thus:

> Down by yon valley gardens
> One evening as I chanced to stray
> It's there I saw my darling,
> I took her to be the Queen of May.
> She told me to take love easy
> Just as the leaves grow on the tree,
> But I being young and foolish
> Her then I did not agree.

Observe how the genius of W. B. Yeats has transmuted it.'

Despite Henderson's derogatory comment, the folk version is so much superior to most broadside texts that it seems likely it was a folk song before it fell into the hands of the broadside printers.

In *Ballads Migrant in New England* (123) Mrs Flanders gives a text from a copy book 'handwritten by Joseph Goffe, dated 1784 in Bedford, New Hampshire'. Helen Creighton got a related song, *Rambling Rover*, from Ben Henneberry (SBNS 95), and another from Mr Doran (FSNB 117). Carrie Grover has one called *Sally's Garden* with a similar first verse (12). In Ireland Sean O'Boyle collected a version from Robert Cinnamond that is most similar to the Ontario text: Paddy Tunney sings it on Topic 12T165.

60. *An Old Man He Courted Me*
Fowke TSSO 32
(Prestige/International 25014)

The young girl who weds an old man is the subject of many ballads, but this one seems to be the most popular in British tradition. It first appeared in

Herd's *Ancient and Modern Scottish Songs* in 1776 as *Scant of Love, Want of Love* (appendix 63), and has been recorded in modern times by Jeannie Robertson (Caedmon TC 1143) and Willie MacPhee (Prestige/International 25016). In England Kidson printed a stanza in *Traditional Tunes* (92) in 1891, and in 1906 the air of another version noted in Yorkshire (JFSS II 273). More recently Peggy Seeger and Ewan MacColl recorded it from Sam Larner of Norfolk (Folkways FG 3507). Joyce found it in Ireland (AIM 111), and Mr Abbott learned his around 1895 from Johnny Hopewell who came out from Ireland to farm in the Ottawa Valley. Only two other versions have turned up on this continent: Hubbard gives a shorter form in *Ballads and Songs from Utah* (156), and Edna Ritchie has recorded a rather mild form on Folk Legacy FSA 3.

61. *The Weaver*
Fowke TSSO 38
(Prestige/International 25014)

This much rarer ballad Mr Abbott learned from Dan Leahy, an Irish farm labourer, in Marchurst, Ontario, around 1890, when Leahy would have been about seventy. It has not been reported from oral tradition elsewhere, but a ten-stanza version appears in the nineteenth-century Jones-Conklin manuscript of an American sailor which Kenneth S. Goldstein is preparing for publication. The song apparently dates from the pre-industrial era when handloom weavers travelled from town to town weaving the yarn that housewives had spun. Both 'the Rose and the Crown' and 'the Diamond Twill' are traditional patterns listed in a British dictionary of the weaving trade.

62. *Nellie Coming Home from the Wake*
   Fowke TSSO 36
   (Folkways FM 4051)

Another of Mr Abbott's fine songs, this is much better known than *The Weaver*, although it has rarely appeared in print. Harry Cox recorded it for the BBC, and H. P. Beck reports a version from Maine under the title of *Ramble Away* (184). The Ottawa singer Tom Kines, who has recorded Mr Abbott's version (Folkways FG 3522), notes that the tune 'has the rhythm of a high-stepping pony hitched to a jaunting car'.

63. *She's like the Swallow*
   Peacock 711

This is a distinctive Newfoundland variant of a large family of songs about unhappy love of which *A Brisk Young Sailor*, *Must I Go Bound* and *Died for Love* (Dean-Smith 63) are the best known. Maud Karpeles noted it first in 1930 (243), and Peacock found two versions some thirty years later. I collected still another version in Ontario from the former Newfoundlander, Albert Simms (TSSO 147).

The swallow simile seems to be found only in Newfoundland, but the other verses turn up in various songs. Peacock notes that a song written by Robert Johnson, a poet born in 1659, contains a close parallel to the verse about the flowery bed, and Karpeles cites an unpublished version noted by Cecil Sharp that parallels verses two and four.

64. *The Bonny Bunch of Rushes Green*
   O. J. Abbott, Hull, Quebec, 1957
   (FO 1-8)

This is an English version of the widely known Irish Gaelic song, *An Beinsin Luachra* (*The Little Bench of Rushes*) which Maire O'Sullivan sings on Columbia SL 204. In *Reliques of Irish Jacobite Poetry* O'Daly explains:

> The meaning of the word '*beinsin*' (little bench) is mistaken by some of our most eminent writers, who suppose it to mean a 'bunch'. In your youthful days it was a general custom with the peasantry to go on Midsummer Eve to the next bog, and cut a '*beart luachra*' (bundle of rushes), as much as a stout lad could carry home on his back; and this they strewed on benches of stone made for the purpose inside and outside their cottages; where the youth of the neighbourhood spent the evening in the usual pastimes.

The original ballad follows the familiar pattern of the maid seduced and deserted, but Mr Abbott turns it into a song celebrating the delights of true love. In JFSS III 17 Lucy Broadwood gives a version from Waterford, Ireland, with alternate English and Gaelic stanzas. She mentions 'a balladsheet printed by Such, *The Bunch of Rushes*, which is evidently a paraphrase of a common Irish original, but it is distinct from the Irish ballad here printed,' and another version collected by H. E. D. Hammond in 1905. In *The Everlasting Circle* (118) James Reeves gives one Gardiner collected in Southampton that is based on a still different translation, and Brocklebank gives another from Dorset (28). Sam Henry has a similar song, *The Tossing of the Hay* (No. 635). None of these has anything corresponding to Mr Abbott's final stanza, which suggests that he may have added it himself. The only previous trace of it in North America seems to be a fragment that Helen Creighton got from Angelo Dornan (FSNB 54).

65. *The Sailor's Return* (N 42)
   C. H. J. Snider, Toronto, 1960
   (FO 9-79)

Of the many ballads on the broken ring theme, this is the most popular in Canada. It has been sung in much the same form all through Britain, Canada and the United States under such titles as *The Young and Single Sailor*, *The Broken Token*, *A Pretty Fair Maid* or *A Fair Maid Walked in Her Father's Garden*. This Ontario version follows the usual pattern except that its reference to a castle is rare in England and America, although it is found in Scotland. Mr Snider learned this in Picton, Ontario, in 1944 from a Great Lakes sailor named Henry McConnell, then eighty-five, who used to sing in dockside bars for whisky.

In addition to the many American versions Laws gives (ABBB 224), it is in CFB II 24, Creighton MFS 59, Fuson 77, and Peacock 584. For English versions see Dean-Smith 55 and add Brocklebank 17 and Reeves 64. Irish versions include Henry Nos. 471 and 818 and Hughes IV 63. Traditional recordings include Elizabeth Cronin and Jean Ritchie (Collector 1201), Roscoe Holcomb (Folkways FA 2390), Mrs Towns (Folkways FM 4005), Maud Long (Library of Congress AAFS L 21), John P. Bashears (Louisiana Folklore Society LFS 1201) and Jeannie Robertson (Riverside RLP 12-633).

66. *The Plains of Waterloo* (N 32)
   Fowke TSSO 54
   (Folkways FM 4051)

This fine version of the broken ring story seems to be best known in Canada. Dr Mackenzie, the first to report it (183), suggests that it is a modified version of *The Mantle So Green* (N 38), which in its turn is a modified version of the eighteenth-century *George Reilly* (N 36). Creighton found three more versions in Nova Scotia (MFS 56 and Folkways FE 4307); Greenleaf (172) and Peacock (1014) found it in Newfoundland; Leach in Labrador (172); Creighton in New Brunswick (FSNB 76); and I have two other versions from Ontario.

67. *Will O'Riley* (M 8)
   Dave McMahon, Douro, 1957
   (FO 13-127)

The Rileys have inspired more than their share of ballads. In addition to this lovers' tragedy caused by parental opposition, the girl's father causes 'Willie Riley' to be imprisoned in two others (M 9 and M 10); two returned lover ballads take their title from their hero, *John Riley* or *George Riley* (N 36 and N 37), and another, *The Mantle So Green* (N 38), has a Will O' Riley as its hero. (G. Malcolm Laws discusses the Riley ballads in *Folklore in Action*, edited by H. P. Beck, 172-83). All of these have been sung in Canada, and this one is the most popular in Nova Scotia, Newfoundland and Ontario. In addition to the references Laws gives (ABBB 184), it is in Creighton MFS 102 and FSNB 133, Karpeles 163, Leach 58 and Peacock 698, and there is a Nova Scotia version on Folkways FE 4307. England has half a dozen versions (Dean-Smith 81), and Scotland and Ireland several, usually as *John Riley* or *Young Riley the Fisherman*. It was also a favourite of the broadside printers.

Most of the traditional versions are quite similar, and Mr McMahon's text follows the usual pattern except for the first half of stanza 7 which normally runs:

> And it's then twelve months after she
>   was walking by the sea

When Riley he came back again and
took his love away.

In its travels through the Canadian
lumber woods the ballad somewhere
lost one twist of the plot, and thus fails
to make clear how the two lovers came
to be on board the same ship. In place
of these two lines, a description of the
storm that wrecked the ship has been
substituted.

68. The Green Brier Shore
Leo Spencer, Lakefield, 1962

This is an excellent example of how
new ballads were re-created from the
floating stanzas of old ones. As it
stands, it is a fairly consistent story:
a man falls in love with a rich girl who
loves him in return and promises to
elope with him despite her parents'
opposition. In this form I have not
found it elsewhere, but it borrows
stanzas from at least two better known
broadsides. The first two correspond
to those usually found in the more
widespread Green Brier Shore (M 26).
That ballad itself is a composite of
elements found in other songs, as
Mackenzie has shown (137), but it
normally tells how the hero battles
armed men whom the girl's father has
hired to kill him. Mr Spencer's third,
fourth and fifth stanzas are not in-
consistent with this story although they
are not found in other versions. His
last stanza seems to have been borrowed from a completely different
ballad, Lovely Willie (M 35), which
tells how the girl's father catches the
lovers when they meet in the garden,
and kills the young man. It is strange
to find a stanza from a tragic ballad
used as the climax of a completely
different ballad to suggest a happy
ending.

69. The Bonny Labouring Boy (M 14)
Leo Spencer, Lakefield, 1962

This tale of the girl who loved The
Bonny Labouring Boy provided the
pattern for two native Ontario variants: My Jolly Shantyboy (Fowke
LSNW 192) and The Jolly Railroad Boy
(Folkways FM 4005). The original is
not very common in North America:
Karpeles (216) and Peacock (564)
found it in Newfoundland, and
Gardner in Indiana (180). It was more
popular in England, turning up in
Surrey, Hampshire and Dorset (Dean-
Smith 54 and Brocklebank 4). Both
Henry (No. 576) and Hughes (IV 59)
found it in Ireland. Harry Cox has
recorded it on Folk Legacy FSB 20. It
appeared on many nineteenth-century
ballad sheets, and Mr Spencer's text
is close to a Such broadside given in
JFSS I 206, except that in it the couple
flee to Plymouth rather than Belfast.

70. The Ship's Carpenter (P 36A)
Leo Spencer, Lakefield, 1962
(FO 14-134)

The girl betrayed and murdered is almost as popular a ballad plot as that
happier tale of the lover returning in
disguise. This one stems from The
Gosport Tragedy, or, Perjured Ship
Carpenter, a garland printed in London
around 1750. Its thirty-five stanzas
were later condensed into an eleven-
stanza broadside known as Polly's
Love, or, The Cruel Ship Carpenter, of
which Frank Kidson wrote in 1901:
'Few ballads are more popular with
ballad-printers than this. It is sung to
different tunes throughout England'
(JFSS I 173). (For English versions
see Dean-Smith 61 and Folkways FH
3507.) It is also widely sung in North
America, but the most popular form
in the United States is a still shorter
version known as Pretty Polly (P36B)

which ends with the murder. In Canada the older form seems to have been preferred. (To Laws ABBB 268 add Grover 43, Hubbard 60, Karpeles 115, Manny 387 and Peacock 404.)

Although Mr Spencer's nineteen stanzas took thirteen minutes to sing, his version is still short compared to the original thirty-five stanzas.

71. *Jamie Foyer*
    Mrs A. Fraser, Lancaster, 1962

This is an abbreviated version of the Scottish ballad about *Young Jamie Foyers* who died in the Napoleonic War. In 1904 when Robert Ford printed it in *Vagabond Songs and Ballads of Scotland* (18), he noted:

This typical bothy ballad, which perhaps appears in a book now for the first time, was a prime favourite at the harvest homes, foys, and Handsel-Monday gatherings in the rural parts of Perthshire before and about the middle of the last century. Like the ballads of olden time generally, its story in the main is presumably based on a matter of fact, so that one Jamie Foyers, from the Perthshire Militia, went out under the 'Iron Duke' to fight the French in Portugal and Spain in 1810, and, as the reward for his heroism, met the fate accorded to him in the verses, may be accepted freely as a bit of real history ... The ballad itself I copied thirty years before from the singing of a Perthshire woman, who died in 1899. The writer in the *Glasgow Weekly Herald* names one John M'Neill as the author.

Ewan MacColl, who revised *Young Jamie Foyers* to tell of a young Scotsman dying in the Spanish Civil War, says that it was also sung during the Boer War and the African Zulu War. Ord (294) gives it as a bothy song, and Kenneth S. Goldstein reports that it is

one of the most popular songs in north-eastern Scotland today. On this continent it seems to be remembered only in Canada: Edward Ives found three versions in New Brunswick (NEF I 10), and Helen Creighton found another (FSNB 208). As the ballad originally had ten stanzas, Mrs Fraser's version is little more than a fragment, but the lines she does remember are those that describe the action and actually tell a fairly complete story.

72. *The Banks of the Nile* (N 9)
    LaRena Clark, Toronto, 1961
    (Topic 12T140)

Ballads about a girl dressing in men's clothes to follow her lover to sea or to war are almost as numerous as the broken ring ballads – Laws lists seventeen (N 1 to N 17), most of which have turned up in Canada. *The Banks of the Nile* is an offshoot of an older ballad, *William and Nancy* (N 8), and an early form, *The Undaunted Seaman, who resolved to fight for his King and Country: Together with His Love's Sorrowful Lamentation at their Departure*, dates from about 1690. It was re-written a century later to apply to the British campaign against Napoleon in Egypt. In its turn, *The Banks of the Nile* took new forms on two other continents: in North America to describe Union soldiers going to fight the Southerners, as *Dixie's Isle* (Mackenzie 113), and in Australia to describe the shearers going to sheep stations on *The Banks of the Condamine* or *The Banks of Riverine* (Wattle Archive Series 2).

In North America it has survived in Missouri and Minnesota (Laws ABBB 207) and Michigan (Gardner 171), as well as in Newfoundland (Peacock 996) and Nova Scotia (Creighton MFS 147, Mackenzie 111).

Sidney Richards sings an English version on Caedmon TC 1164. Mrs Clark's version, which she learned from her Grandad Watson, is closer to the British texts than the other American versions. The last stanza is a neat localizing of the older form, and the second to last line suggests it has passed through Irish lips, where 'soil' would be pronounced 's'ile', as in a version given by Sam Henry (No. 238).

73. *Nine Years a Soldier* (J 8)
Stanley James, Weston, 1957

This tale of the Irish farm lad who enlisted in the British army was very popular in Ontario, and both Creighton (MFS 162) and Fauset (120) found it in Nova Scotia. In the United States it has been reported from Michigan and Kentucky (Laws ABBB 132), Pennsylvania (Shoemaker 219), Georgia (M. E. Henry 402) and Missouri (Randolph III 240). Con Skully sings it on Folkways FW 8872, and William Rew on Caedmon TC 1164. It was more common on broadsides and songsters, usually as *The Kerry Recruit*, and often with references to the Crimean War. All versions tell how the lad is fitted out with an overcoat, a gun and a horse, and all have a nonsense refrain – and most of the refrains are different. The reference to Vinegar Hill in Mr James's version suggests that it dates back to the Irish rebellion of 1798. The phrase, 'Give a soldier your fist' sometimes runs: 'Stick a bob in my fist' – a reference to the King's shilling given to new recruits.

74. *The Enniskillen Dragoon*
C. H. J. Snider, Toronto, 1961

This song is well known in Ireland but it has rarely been reported from tradition in North America, although it was fairly common in Irish-American songsters. Mrs Eddy found the first stanza in Ohio (316); Oscar Brand learned it from an Irish family (Folkways FA 2428); and Helen Creighton has an unpublished version in her collection. Mr Snider learned it from his mother who got it from her grandmother, Molly Mahaffey, who was born in Donegal in 1790 and came out to Canada in 1837.

In Ireland Dr Joyce, who was the first to report it (OIFMS 208), notes:

This song, though of Ulster origin, was a great favourite in Munster where I learned it when I was very young; it was indeed sung all over Ireland. I published the words more than fifty years ago in a newspaper called *The Tipperary Leader*, and I have several copies printed on ballad sheets. Some few years ago I gave a copy of the air as I had it in memory to Dr Sigerson who wrote a new song to it which was published in Mr A. P. Graves' *Irish Song Book* and in that publication so far as I know the air appeared in print for the first time.

Sam Henry also found it (Nos. 98 and 630), and Ord reports it from Scotland (306).

75. *The Farmer and the Devil* (Child 278)
Michael Cuddihey, Low, Quebec, 1957 (FO 17-159)

Tales of a woman who is a terror to demons are common in the folklore of both Europe and Asia, and ballads on this theme have been known in England since the Elizabethan age when a broadside called *The Devil and the Scold* was printed. It was already popular in Scotland by the time of Burns, for his *Kellyburnbraes* was fashioned 'from the old traditional version', and it appeared on many nineteenth-century broadsides. It has continued remarkably popular up to the present.

Mrs Cuddihey's version, learned in the northern Ontario lumber woods, follows the pattern of the Sussex text given as Child A, complete to the whistled refrain that caused it to be known as the *Sussex Whistling Song*. It is unusual for one version to have both the whistled refrain, found in most English versions, and a nonsense refrain, more popular in America. For references see Coffin 148, Dean-Smith 66, and add Peacock 265 and Moore 127. Traditional recorded versions include Estil Ball (Atlantic 1346), Paddy Moran (Caedmon TC 1146), Edna Ritchie (Folk Legacy FSA 3), Lawrence Older (Folk Legacy FSA 15), Hobart Smith (Folk Legacy FSA 17), Len Armstrong and Ella Jones (Folk Legacy FSA 22), Horton Barker (Folkways FA 2362 and Library of Congress AAFS L 1), Bill and Belle Reed (Folkways FA 2951), Carrie Grover (AAFS L 58), Harry Duffy (Prestige / International 25016), James Cottrell (Vanguard VRS 9147).

76. *Seven Gypsies on yon Hill*
(Child 200)
Robert Campbell, Weston, 1962

This comes closer to the original Scottish form of *The Gypsy Laddie* than any previously reported North American version. It follows the older pattern in telling of a band of gypsies who stole a lord's lady and were finally captured and hanged; and its mention of Lord Castle harks back to the Scottish texts about Lord Cassilis. Most American texts speak of a single gypsy and lack the tragic ending, although Text J in Flanders' *Ancient Ballads Traditionally Sung in New England* has the lord killing both his wife and the gypsy. On the whole Mr Campbell's text compares most closely to Child G from the Roxburghe Ballads, although the conversation with the old man compares with the meeting 'wi' a cheel' in E 12-13, and stanzas 8 and 13 are paralleled most closely by Child 1, 5 and 2.

Mr Campbell says he learned this ballad from his mother. His maternal great-grandfather came out from Ireland in the early part of the nineteenth century and probably brought the ballad with him. *The Journal of the Irish Folk Song Society* (I 42) prints a very similar text as *The Dark Eyed Gypsy O* and Sam Henry has it as *The Brown Eyed Gypsies* (No. 24) in which the lord 'rode from Strabogie O'.

Two traditional versions from Donegal and Derry are included on Leader LEA 4055.

The popularity of this ballad is indicated by the fact that Bronson gives 128 versions (III 198); for another Ontario version see Fowke TSSO 18.

77. *The Dewy Dells of Yarrow*
(Child 214)
John A. MacDonald, Cornwall, 1961
(FO 23-216)

This ancient Scottish ballad is rare on this continent, and Mr MacDonald's version is fuller and closer to the Child texts than other North American versions. It is made up of stanzas he sang in 1961 pieced out by stanzas supplied in manuscript by Mrs MacDonald. Despite several attempts (and much prompting by his wife), Mr MacDonald was unable to sing the complete ballad at that time, but Mrs MacDonald says the version given is the way he used to sing it. He learned it from one of the men with whom he worked in his youth some forty years ago. Nine of the stanzas correspond fairly closely to Child Q, but stanzas like 5 and 6 appear only in the older Child A-E group, with E 6-7 providing the closest parallel. On the whole Mr MacDonald's text is very similar to one sung by the fine traditional Scottish singer Davy Stewart on Caedmon TC 1146. For a slightly different form of the ballad sung by Mr MacDonald's sister-in-law and references, see TSSO 52 and 173. The only other Canadian report is a fragmentary version from Newfoundland (Karpeles 95). For Scottish and American versions see Bronson III 314.

78. *Willie Drowned in Ero*
(Child 215)
Mrs Eva Bigrow, Calumet, Quebec, 1964

The ballad that Child lists as *Rare Willie Drowned in Yarrow, or The Water o' Gamrie* is much rarer in tradition than *The Braes o' Yarrow*, and existing versions suggest that the two have been confused. Both Child (IV 178) and Coffin (130) point out that they overlap, and Norman Cazden suggests that the first three versions of Child 215, which have the hero drowned in Yarrow, properly belong to *The Braes o' Yarrow*.

Mrs Bigrow's version is more complete than most. She sang the first five stanzas for me in 1964 and sent the last two in a letter dated 11 January 1965. She had learned it as a child in Kilmar, Glengarry, around 1900, from some of her girl friends whose families were Scottish. Another earlier version reported in North America, in Eddy's *Ballads and Songs from Ohio* (69), is similar to this in text and structure but lacks stanzas 4 and 7. The Canadian version is close to Child C, but it differs from other texts in having stanza 5 in the first person, and the last stanza may be a local addition for nothing like it appears elsewhere. The other stanzas parallel these known by the Arkansas singer, Almeda Riddle (Abrahams 124). For

Scottish versions see Bronson III 328 and Ord 454.

79. *Jenny Go Gentle*
(Child 277)
Stanley James, Weston, 1957
(FO 17-161)

Dr Child, who lists this ballad as *The Wife Wrapt in Wether's Skin*, suggests that it comes from a sixteenth-century metrical tale: *A merry jeste of a shrewde and curste wyfe lapped in Morrelles skin for her good behauyour.* The five versions he gives are all Scottish, resembling *The Wee Cooper of Fife*. A version in his appendix (V 304) collected in Massachusetts early in the nineteenth century seems to be the ancestor of this Ontario song. Mr James's omitted stanzas describing the wife's failings and also the ending in which she threatens to tell her family and finally reforms, but his shortened version is still coherent and well rounded. Its refrain shows the effect of oral tradition on the old plant burden, 'Juniper, gentian and rosemary', which is said to have been a charm providing protection against demons. Professor Belden (92) suggests that the rosemary refrain was borrowed from *The Elfin Knight* (Child 2), and that it is the most common form in the southern and north-eastern states. For other versions, refer to Coffin 146 and Bronson IV, 143. It has been recorded by Edna Ritchie (Folk Legacy FSA 3), Jean Ritchie (Folkways FA 2302), Frank Proffitt (Folkways FA 2360) and David Lewis (Louisiana Folklore Society LSF 1202).

80. *The Footboy*
Emerson Woodcock, Peterborough, 1958 (FO 13-132)

This ballad is puzzling: I have been unable to find it in any traditional collection in either Britain or North America, or in any broadside collection. It contains elements suggesting various known broadsides: the father who tries to prevent his daughter marrying a servant is common in the ballads of 'Family Opposition to Lovers', and the device of planting items on the lover so he can be accused of robbery occurs in such songs as *William Riley* (M 10), *Henry Connors* (M 5) and *Mary Acklin* (M 16). But in none of these is the lover hanged: at worst he is transported or imprisoned, although usually his sweetheart manages to free him.

The form and style of *The Footboy* seem closer to the popular ballads than to the broadsides. It uses a common ballad metre and a type of repetition more often found in older ballads. The fact that the lover is hanged also suggests that it dates from an earlier period than those in which he is transported, and the term 'footboy' for a young manservant has a medieval flavour: it was in common use at the time of Shakespeare but had largely disappeared by the nineteenth century.

81. *The House Carpenter* (Child 243)
LaRena Clark, Toronto, 1961
(Topic 12T140)

The earliest version of this ballad was in the Pepys collection as *A Warning for Married Women, being an example of Jane Reynolds (a West Country woman), born near Plymouth, who plighted her troth to a Seaman, was afterwards married to a Carpenter, and at last carried away by a Spirit.* Child gives this and seven other versions apparently derived from it under the title of *James Harris (The Daemon Lover)* (IV 360) and mentions that 'An Americanized version of this ballad was printed not very long ago at Philadelphia, under the title of *The House-Carpenter.*' This and a similar broadside printed by DeMarsan in New York about 1860 set the pattern for most versions reported from tradition in the last century.

Although it is rather rare in Britain (Dean-Smith 80), this ballad has been very widely sung in America and appears in most major collections. Singers on this continent tend to drop the supernatural elements and simplify the plot. Although most versions tell the same story in much the same way, the endings show considerable variety. Mrs Clark's ending, in which the girl throws herself overboard, is classified by Coffin as Type D (137), and conforms most closely to a text found by Mrs Eddy in Ohio (70, A). In addition to the voluminous references Bronson gives (III 429), Peacock has a Newfoundland version (740).

82. *The 'Green Willow Tree'* (Child 286)
Fowke TSSO 156 (FO 17-160)

The old British sea ballad of *The 'Golden Vanity'* or *The 'Sweet Trinity'* was very popular in Canada: Creighton gives one version in SBNS (20) and five in TSNS (101); Grover has another Nova Scotia version (176); Greenleaf (143) and Karpeles (107) found it in Newfoundland, and Leach in Labrador (44); Creighton gives two versions from New Brunswick (FSNB 17), and I have two other Ontario versions (TSSO 20, and Folkways FM 4052). (For other references see Bronson IV, 312.)

This version from Stanley James is unusually complete, and closer to the Child texts than most North American versions. The reference to the boy being wrapped in a 'black bull-skin' corresponds to Child B: a version given in JFSS II 244 in 1906 mentions a 'black bear-skin', which the singer explained was the boy's covering at night, worn as a disguise in the water.

INDEX OF TITLES AND FIRST LINES

BIBLIOGRAPHY

Asterisks indicate books from which songs have been reprinted.

ABRAHAMS, Roger (ed.), *A Singer and Her Songs: Almeda Riddle's Book of Ballads*, Baton Rouge, 1970.

BARBEAU, Marius, *Alouette*, Montreal, 1946.

BARBEAU, Marius, *Jongleur Songs of Old Quebec*, New Brunswick, N.J., and Toronto, 1962.

*BARBEAU, Marius, Arthur Lismer and Arthur Bourinot, *Come A-Singing!*, Ottawa, 1947.

BECK, Earl Clifton, *Lore of the Lumber Camps*, Ann Arbor, Mich., 1948.

BECK, Horace P., *The Folklore of Maine*, Philadelphia and New York, 1957.

BELDEN, Henry Marvin, *Ballads and Songs Collected by the Missouri Folk-Lore Society*, Columbia, Mo., 1940.

BROCKLEBANK, Joan, and Biddie Kindersley, *A Dorset Book of Folk Songs*, London, 1948.

BRONSON, Bertrand Harris, *The Traditional Tunes of the Child Ballads*, 4 vols., Princetown, N.J., 1959-72.

BROWN, *The Frank C. Brown Collection of North Carolina Folklore*, vol. III, Durham, N.C., 1952.

*CASS-BEGGS, Barbara, *Seven Metis Songs of Saskatchewan*, Toronto, 1967.

CFB: *Colorado Folksong Bulletin*, Boulder, Colo., 1962-

CHILD, Francis James, *The English and Scottish Popular Ballads*, 5 vols., Boston and New York, 1882-98; reprinted New York, 1956.

COFFIN, Tristram P., *The British Traditional Ballad in North America*, Philadelphia, 1963.

COLCORD, Joanna C., *Songs of American Sailormen*, New York, 1938.

COMBS, Josiah H., *Folk-Songs of the Southern United States*, ed. D. K. Wilgus, Austin, Texas, and London, 1967.

COX, John Harrington, *Folk-Songs of the South*, Cambridge, Mass., 1925.

CREIGHTON, Helen, *Folksongs from Southern New Brunswick*, Ottawa, 1971.

CREIGHTON, Helen, *Maritime Folk Songs*, Toronto, 1962.

CREIGHTON, Helen, *Songs and Ballads from Nova Scotia*, Toronto, 1932.

*CREIGHTON, Helen, and Doreen H. Senior, *Traditional Songs from Nova Scotia*, Toronto, 1950.

DEAN-SMITH, Margaret, *A Guide to English Folk Song Collections 1822-1952*, Liverpool, 1954.

DOERFLINGER, William Main, *Shantymen and Shantyboys*, New York, 1951.

*DOYLE, Gerald S., *The Old Time Songs and Poetry of Newfoundland*, St John's, 1927, 1940, 1955, 1966.

ECKSTORM, Fannie Hardy, and Mary Winslow Smyth, *Minstrelsy of Maine*, Boston, 1927.

EDDY, Mary O., *Ballads and Songs from Ohio*, New York, 1931.

FAUSET, Arthur H., *Folklore from Nova Scotia*, New York, 1931.

FLANDERS, Helen Hartness, *Ancient Ballads Traditionally Sung in New England*, 3 vols., Philadelphia, 1960-63.

FLANDERS, Helen Hartness, and Marguerite Olney, *Ballads Migrant in New England*, New York, 1953.

FORD, Robert, *Vagabond Songs and Ballads of Scotland*, Paisley, 1904.

*FOWKE, Edith, *Lumbering Songs from the Northern Woods*, Austin, Texas, 1970.

*FOWKE, Edith, *Traditional Singers and Songs from Ontario*, Hatboro, Penn., 1965.

*FOWKE, Edith, and Alan Mills, *Canada's Story in Song*, Toronto, 1960.

*FOWKE, Edith, and Richard Johnston, *Folk Songs of Canada*, Waterloo, Ont., 1954.

*FOWKE, Edith, and Richard Johnston, *More Folk Songs of Canada*, Waterloo, Ont., 1967.

FUSON, Henry H., *Ballads of the Kentucky Highlands*, London, 1931.

*GAGNON, Ernest., *Chansons populaires du Canada*, Montreal, 1865.

GARDNER, Emelyn E., and Geraldine J. Chickering, *Ballads and Songs of Michigan*, Ann Arbor, Mich., 1937.

GORDON, Robert Winslow, Manuscript Collection in the Archive of American Folk Song, Library of Congress, Washington, D.C.

*GREENLEAF, Elisabeth B., and Grace Y. Mansfield, *Ballads and Sea Songs of Newfoundland*, Cambridge, Mass., 1963.

GROVER, Carrie B., *A Heritage of Songs*, Bethel, Me., n.d.

HENDERSON, W., *Victorian Street Ballads*, London and New York, 1938.

HENRY, M. E., *Songs Sung in the Southern Appalachians*, London, 1934.

HUBBARD, Lester A., *Ballads and Songs from Utah*, Salt Lake City, 1961

HENRY, Sam, 'Songs of the People', Belfast, Ireland, 1923-39.

HUGHES, Herbert, *Irish Country Songs*, 4 vols., London, 1915.

JAF: *Journal of American Folklore*, 1888- .

JEFDSS: *Journal of the English Folk Dance and Song Society*, London, 1932- .

JFSS: *Journal of the Folk Song Society*, London, 1899-1931.

JIFSS: *Journal of the Irish Folk Song Society*, London, 1904-39.

JOYCE, Patrick Weston, *Ancient Irish Music*, Dublin, 1912.

JOYCE, Patrick Weston, *Old Irish Folk Music and Song*, Dublin, 1909.

KARPELES, Maud, *Folk Songs from Newfoundland*, London, 1971.

KORSON, George, *Pennsylvania Songs and Legends*, Philadelphia, 1949.

LAWS, G. Malcolm, Jr, *American Balladry from British Broadsides*, Philadelphia, 1957.

LAWS, G. Malcolm, Jr, *Native American Balladry*, Philadelphia, 1964.

LEACH, MacEdward, *Folk Ballads and Songs of the Lower Labrador Coast*, Ottawa, 1965.

LOMAX, John A., *Cowboy Songs and Other Frontier Ballads*, New York, 1916.

MACDONALD, Alphonse, *Cape Breton Songster*, Sydney, N.S., 1935.

MACKENZIE, W. Roy, *Ballads and Sea Songs from Nova Scotia*, Cambridge, Mass., 1928.

*MANNY, Louise, and J. R. Wilson, *Songs of Miramichi*, Fredericton, N.B., 1968.

*McCAWLEY, Stuart, *Cape Breton Come-All-Ye*, Glace Bay, N.S., 1929.

*MILLS, Alan, *Chantons un peu*, Toronto, 1961.

MOORE, Ethel, and Chauncey O. Moore, *Ballads and Folk Songs of the Southwest*, Norman, Okla., 1964.

MURPHY, James, *Old Songs of Newfoundland*, St John's, 1912.

NEF: *Northeast Folklore*, Orono, Me., 1958- .

ORD, John, *The Bothy Songs and Ballads*, Paisley, 1930.

*PEACOCK, Kenneth, *Songs of the Newfoundland Outports*, 3 vols., Ottawa, 1965.

RANDOLPH, Vance, *Ozark Folksongs*, 4 vols., Columbia, Mo., 1946-50.

REEVES, James, *The Everlasting Circle*, London, 1960.

RICKABY, Franz, *Ballads and Songs of the Shanty-Boy*, Cambridge, Mass., 1926.

SHARP, Cecil, *English Folk-Songs from the Southern Appalachians*, 2 vols., London, 1932.

SHOEMAKER, Henry W., *Mountain Minstrelsy of Pennsylvania*, Philadelphia, 1931.

VINCENT, Elmore, *Lumberjack Songs*, Chicago, 1932.

DISCOGRAPHY

Asterisked records contain songs in this book. In addition, nos. 9, 10, 21, 28, 33, 50, 51, 53, 54, 57, 61, 64, 66, 76, 78 and 80 may be heard on LEADER LEE *4057.*

ATLANTIC 1346, *Sounds of the South*, Southern Folk Heritage Series, Vol. I. Recorded by Alan Lomax.

CAEDMON TC 1143, *Songs of Seduction*, and CAEDMON 1146, *Child Ballads, II*, The Folksongs of Britain, Vols. 2 and 5. Collected and edited by Peter Kennedy and Alan Lomax.

COLLECTOR LIMITED EDITION 1201, *Field Trip*. Recorded by Jean Ritchie and George Pickow.

COLUMBIA KL 204, *Irish Folk Songs*, Columbia World Library of Folk and Primitive Music, Vol. 1. Edited by Seamus Ennis and Alan Lomax.

FOLK LEGACY FSA 1, *Frank Proffitt of Reese, North Carolina.*

FOLK LEGACY FSA 3, *Edna Ritchie of Viper, Kentucky.*

FOLK LEGACY FSC 9, *Marie Hare of Strathadam, New Brunswick, Canada.*

*FOLK LEGACY FSC 10, *Tom Brandon of Peterborough, Ontario, Canada.*

FOLK LEGACY FSA 11, *Max Hunter of Springfield, Missouri.*

FOLK LEGACY FSA 15, *Lawrence Older of Middle Grove, New York.*

FOLK LEGACY FSA 17, *Hobart Smith of Saltville, Virginia.*

FOLK LEGACY FSA 22, *The Traditional Music of Beech Mountain, North Carolina, Vol. I.* Recorded by Sandy Paton.

FOLKWAYS FA 2301-2302, *British Traditional Ballads (Child Ballads) in the Southern Mountains*, Vols. I and II. Sung by Jean Ritchie.

FOLKWAYS FA 2360, *Frank Proffitt Sings Folk Songs*, and FOLKWAYS FA 2362, *Horton Barker, Traditional Singer.* Recorded by Paton.

FOLKWAYS FA 2390, *Friends of Old-Time Music.* Doc Watson, Hobart Smith.

FOLKWAYS FA 2428, *A Folk Concert in Town Hall, New York.* Jean Ritchie, Oscar Brand, David Sear.

FOLKWAYS FA 2951, *Anthology of American Folk Music*, Vol. 1. Edited by Harry Smith.

FOLKWAYS FG 3507, *Now is the Time for Fishing.* Sam Larner of Winterton, England, recorded by Ewan MacColl and Peggy Seeger.

FOLKWAYS FG 3522, *An Irishman in North America.* Sung by Tom Kines.

FOLKWAYS FM 4001, *Wolf River Songs.* Collected by Cowell.

FOLKWAYS FM 4005, *Folk Songs of Ontario.* Collected by Edith Fowke.

*FOLKWAYS FM 4051, *Irish and British Songs from the Ottawa Valley.* Sung by O. J. Abbott.

*FOLKWAYS FM 4052, *Lumbering Songs from the Ontario Shanties.* Collected by Edith Fowke.

FOLKWAYS FM 4053, *Folk Songs of the Miramichi.* From the Miramichi Folk Festival.

FOLKWAYS FE 4075, *Folk Songs from the Outports of Newfoundland.* Collected by MacEdward Leach.

FOLKWAYS FE 4307, *Maritime Folk Songs.* Collected by Helen Creighton.

*FOLKWAYS FE 4312, *Folksongs of Saskatchewan.* Collected by Barbara Cass-Beggs.

FOLKWAYS FE 4530, *Folk Music U.S.A.* Compiled by Harold Courlander.

FOLKWAYS FH 5273, *Tipple, Loom, and Rail.* Sung by Mike Seeger.

FOLKWAYS FW 8744, *Songs of the Maritimes.* Sung by Alan Mills.

FOLKWAYS FW 8781, *The Older Traditions of Connemara and Claire.* Collected by Samuel B. Charters.

FOLKWAYS FW 8872, *Field Trip—Ireland (As I Roved Out).* Recorded by Jean Ritchie and George Pickow.

LEADER LEA 4055, *Folk Ballads from Donegal and Derry.* Collected by Hugh Shields.

LIBRARY OF CONGRESS AAFS L1, *Anglo-American Ballads.* Edited by Alan Lomax.

LIBRARY OF CONGRESS AAFS L21, *Anglo-American Songs and Ballads.* Edited by Duncan B. M. Emrich.

LIBRARY OF CONGRESS AAFS L58, *Child Ballads Traditional in the United States* (II). Edited by Bertrand H. Bronson.

LOUISIANA FOLKLORE SOCIETY LSF 1201, *A Sampler of Louisiana Folksongs.* Collected by Harry Oster.

*PRESTIGE/INTERNATIONAL 25014, *Ontario Ballads and Folksongs.* Collected by Edith Fowke.

PRESTIGE/INTERNATIONAL 25016, *Folksongs and Music from the Berryfields of Blair.* Recorded by Hamish Henderson.

RIVERSIDE RLP 12-633, *Songs of a Scots Tinker Lady.* Sung by Jeannie Robertson.

TOPIC 12T96, *Jeannie Robertson.*

TOPIC 12T165, *Paddy Tunney: The Irish Edge.*

TOPIC 12T174, *Leviathan! Ballads and Songs of the Whaling Trade.* Sung by A. L. Lloyd.

* TOPIC 12T140, *A Canadian Garland.* Sung by LaRena Clark.

VANGUARD VRS 9147, *Old Time Music at Newport.*

VANGUARD VRS 9158, *Almeda Riddle: Songs and Ballads of the Ozarks.*